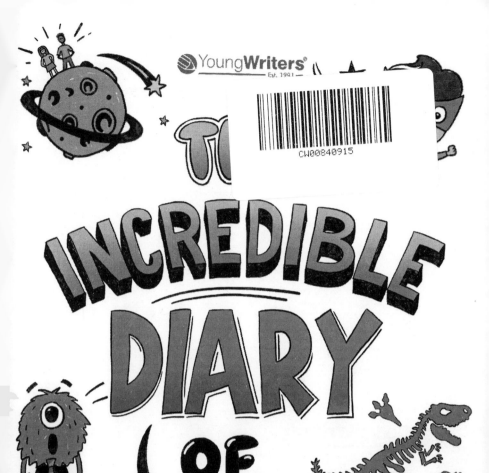

THE INCREDIBLE DIARY OF...

Magical Adventures

Edited By Andy Porter

YoungWriters®
Est. 1991

CW00840915

First published in Great Britain in 2023 by:

Young Writers
Remus House
Coltsfoot Drive
Peterborough
PE2 9BF
Telephone: 01733 890066
Website: www.youngwriters.co.uk

Printed and bound in the UK by BookPrintingUK
Website: www.bookprintinguk.com
YB0547D

FOREWORD

Dear Diary,

You will never guess what I did today! Shall I tell you? Some primary school pupils wrote some diary entries and I got to read them, and they were EXCELLENT!

Here at Young Writers we created some bright and funky worksheets along with fun and fabulous (and free) resources to help spark ideas and get inspiration flowing. And it clearly worked because WOW!! I can't believe the adventures I've been reading about. Real people, make believe people, dogs and unicorns, even objects like pencils all feature and these diaries all have one thing in common — they are JAM-PACKED with imagination, all squeezed into 100 words!

Here at Young Writers we want to pass our love of the written word onto the next generation and what better way to do that than to celebrate their writing by publishing it in a book! It sets their work free from homework books and notepads and puts it where it deserves to be — **OUT IN THE WORLD!**

Each awesome author in this book should be super proud of themselves, and now they've got proof of their imagination, their ideas and their creativity in black and white, to look back on in years to come!

CONTENTS

Tom Milburn (10)   56
Thomas Kinsey-Jones (7)   57

Grange Park Primary School, Sunderland

Alyssa Graham (9)   58
Lucas Bramley (9)   59
Isaac Hill (8)   60
Esme McGhee (9)   61
Freddie Harrison (8)   62
Isabella Hill-Collings (9)   63
Thomas Raine-Dent (8)   64
JJ Broome (9)   65
Oliver Bussell (8)   66
Summer Daley (8)   67
Jayden Prescott (9)   68
Jake Broomfield (9)   69
Leo Davidson (9)   70
Sadie Stubbs (9)   71
Kayci Preen (9)   72
Evie Playle (8)   73
Lilah Mae Downing (8)   74
Lacey Maw (9)   75
Elliott Potts (9)   76

Noor Ul Islam Primary School, Leyton

Maariyah Jiwani (11)   77
Nusaibah Mirza (10)   78
Maryam Imran (11)   79
Rahmah Salahuddin (11)   80
Ayesha Saeed (10)   81

Roydon Primary School, Roydon

Nancy-Ann Jackson (10)   82
Grace Pearce (11)   83
Isla Betts (8)   84
Lexie Edgar-Ayms (8)   85
Scarlett Apea-Agyei (8)   86
Emily Skulski (10)   87
Abrianna Asiamah (9)   88

Emiah Cull (9)   89
Joe Armitt (9)   90
Lexi Bond (9)   91
Nicole Nikalova (9)   92
Poppy Wilkinson (9)   93
Harry Fairweather (11)   94
Ruby-Mae Tennens (9)   95
Roxy Martin (9)   96
Sophie Haddrick (8)   97

Ryhall CE Academy, Ryhall

Izabella Salisbury (9)   98
Anonymous (9)   99
Rudy Maltby (9)   100
Jacob Allwright (9)   101
Orlaith Heames (9)   102
Lilly-Ella Veasey (9)   103
Ava Lidgley (9)   104
Winston Lambert (8)   105
Agatha Scrivens (9)   106
Holly Tinker (9)   107
Tallulah Sorbi (9)   108
Bella-Rose Ferreira (9)   109
Roman Epps (9)   110
Ava Armstrong (8)   111
Esme Scholes (9)   112
Ellena Burrill (9)   113
Tommy Chiverton (8)   114
Joseph Kettle (8)   115
Aurora Penfold (8)   116
Noah Parnell (9)   117
Ashley Dawkins (9)   118

Springfield Primary Academy, Scartho

Archie Jay (8)   119
Harvey Smart (8)   120
Fearne Scott (7)   121
Summer Laker (8)   122
Ella Pound (8)   123
Aurorae Colley (9)   124
Ada Allan (9)   125

Neave Bouch (8)	126
Violet MacLeod (7)	127
Michael May (9)	128
Martha Cook (8)	129
Olivia Gibson (11)	130
Margot Allan (7)	131
Oscar Saxby (9)	132
Sofia Buckman (9)	133
Casey Goodwin (7)	134
Annabelle Balderson (10)	135
Evie Keeler (9)	136
Phoebe Wheeler (8)	137

St Mary's CE School, Norwood Green

Daniel Stonebridge (10)	138
Millie-Sophia Carter Kapoor (10)	139
Aariya Sanghera (9)	140
Kirsty J Bown (10)	141
Shanae Leo (10)	142
Rayyan Mohammad (10)	143
Isabella Rose (9)	144
Aryan Dhiri (9)	145
Arnav Khandekar (9)	146
Ruby Joao (10)	147
Esther Nang Htun Myo Aye (10)	148
Krish Nahar (10)	149
Zainab Akhter (11)	150
Olivia Grace Parris (10)	151
Kyrie Schutter (10)	152
Leah Rai (10)	153
Chidera Amako (10)	154
Aaryan Mohan	155
Zau Lahkum-Lahpai (11)	156
Mysha Tasiq (11)	157
Anastasia Sauch (10)	158
Eleonora Bahus (10)	159
Samanpreet Singh (10)	160
Samuel Schiattarella (10)	161
Kerab Debela (10)	162
Nathan Streets (10)	163
Amelia-Rose Campbell Peccoo	164
Amaiya Chaudhry (9)	165

Harjas Chopra (9)	166
Daria-Ioana Bobu (10)	167
Kashish Yasin Mistry (11)	168
Nitya Itlas (10)	169
David Daikri (11)	170
Keziah Maqbool (9)	171
Jessica Karolina Kwasnik (9)	172
Zaki Awan (10)	173
Gurnoor Singh (10)	174
Joel Bhatti (11)	175
Limmy Tingneilim Khongsai (11)	176
Devika Thakrar (10)	177
Radhika Kaupau (9)	178
Ethan Hamlyn (9)	179
Rafaella Armond (10)	180
Isla Mustafa (10)	181
Christopher Rodrigues (11)	182
Sukhleen Deoora (11)	183
David Wilson-Paz (10)	184
Jahmala Joseph (11)	185
Harman Chopra (9)	186

The Erme Primary School, Ivybridge

Will J Frude (9)	187
Henry Barons (8)	188
Iyla-Grace Thorne (8)	189
Layla-Mai Britton (8)	190
Harry Turberville (8)	191
Nina Jewell (8)	192
Esmé Holmes (9)	193
Ava Douglas (9)	194
Henry Bailey (8)	195
Elsie Hammond (9)	196
Bella McMillan (7)	197
Issy Croney (7)	198
Freya Harper (7)	199
Owen Rea Riding (8)	200
Harry Hawkins (9)	201

In It To Win It? In It To Have Fun!

Dear Diary,

Today my great-grandad Hatti took me on a traditional boat race on the island, Helgoland. The marina was festively decorated. Fascinated tourists watched the wooden boats compete. I dressed like a pirate, excitedly tying a scary skull bandana around my head. Three, two, one... Our boat, 'Klaus', shot off rapidly! We raced around the first buoy, cutting off our opponents, leaving me amazed. With a final spurt, neck and neck with the boat 'Claudia', we came in second place. At the 'after party', we enjoyed delicious hot dogs, won a silver trophy and danced the night away.

Holly Haycock (7)
Aldbrough Primary School, Aldbrough

The Race Under The Sea

Dear Diary.

Today I, a chestnut-coloured horse was galloping along a grassy field with my herd, and happy until a crack of a whip caught my attention.

Rapidly I dashed back to the herd. I neighed to give a warning, it was too late. They cantered alongside a deep river. I fell into the water, Domino tried to catch me but he couldn't.

We were underwater. Then I opened my mouth to get air. "Wow!" I declared under the sea.

"We can breathe underwater!" exclaimed Domino. I said, "What's that?" An underwater race. I won first! Then we went home.

Leah Treadaway (7)

Aldbrough Primary School, Aldbrough

Rich Fit 2

Dear Diary,

Yesterday the *worst* thing happened to me! I went to school, as usual, but someone found out my secret! I was just sitting down beside Amelia-May, my best friend, when something bizarre happened! I felt someone tugging at my wing! I knew that nobody sat behind me, but sometimes Tilly, the teacher, watched us from behind. I asked if I could go to the loo, and Tilly said yes! I happily skipped to the loo and fluttered my wings. But Harriot, my classmate, saw.

"OMG!" she screamed.

I rushed out of the loo. But Harriot posted it. O-M-Gosh!

Esmé Hayden (9)
Aldbrough Primary School, Aldbrough

Gangster's Party Day

Dear Diary,

Today was epic, but not in an epic way.

I was at Rodrick's party with Mum, Sam and Dad.

So basically, Rodrick and I were playing with our water blasters until Little Worm Sam ran in and started annoying us, so I told him to "Shut it." It seemed a bad idea as Peter shrieked to know-it-all Mum and Dad, and of course, like always, they came. But this time they were savage. Well actually, they're always savage, but they didn't give me a chance.

They just took me home screaming, "It's just not fair!"

Charlie

Aldbrough Primary School, Aldbrough

The... Thing

Dear Diary,

I'm in big trouble! But not the type you'd ever understand. My day started off normal. Brushed my teeth, got dressed and went to school. Mayhem began on the way home! My house was just a street away from school. I was almost home till I stopped! The cutest... *thing* I've ever seen! It was like a fluffy cow-print fuzzball with glimmering eyes! I *had* to take it. I secretly squished it in my school bag, but as soon as it laid foot in my house, it went crazy! My mum's home soon! Any ideas at all?

Lily-May Landon (10)
Aldbrough Primary School, Aldbrough

Little Miss Perfect

Dear Diary,

It's been a usual day as a princess, I got kissed by a prince and a frog, went to the mall and met my friends, got some amazing photos with my fans, and then I got lunch. After I got in my golden carriage, I went to my beautiful castle.

Once inside, I asked the mirror, "Mirror, mirror on the wall, who is the prettiest of them all?"

She said, "Belle," instead of 'Little Miss Perfect'.

I knew I had to get revenge! So I got my notebook out and started planning sweet revenge...

Sienna Larkham (11)

Aldbrough Primary School, Aldbrough

Fireworks For Bobby

Dear Diary,

I've had such a brilliant experience! It all began when I was stalking a mouse, when suddenly the sky lit up and I shoved my paws in my ears. Then I heard lots of squeals and bangs and I went for cover. When my owner brought me inside, I relaxed and she told me they were just fireworks and it was bonfire night. A time to celebrate! She toasted marshmallows over our roaring fire and we watched fireworks from the window. I felt safe sitting on my owner's lap. I will never ever forget my first bonfire night!

Martha-Grace Bateson (8)

Aldbrough Primary School, Aldbrough

My Holiday

Dear Diary,
My last holiday might've actually been my last!
Last summer we went to Texas. It wasn't my first thought, I would've rather stayed at home and played video games but my mum talked me out of it. So we set off the next Saturday. It took a good two hours and forty-six minutes to get from Ohio to Texas, so I slept half the way. When we got to Texas, the first thing I did was swim in the ocean. It was pretty nice until some jellyfish wanted in! Turns out, they were box jellyfish! I could've died!

Riley Hancox (11)
Aldbrough Primary School, Aldbrough

The Fairy And The Naughty Pixie

Dear Diary,

Guess what happened yesterday? I went to get my magic fairy dust, it had disappeared. I was very upset. I was going to sprinkle it over the lanterns for the fairies' summer fair. Diary, I knew who it was! The naughty pixie called Peter.

I went to him and said, "Peter, that's my fairy dust, I can see!"

He laughed and said he took it for a joke. I asked Peter if he would like to help, he said yes, so Peter and I sprinkled the fairy dust on all the lanterns and they lit up the sky.

Ebonie Wells (7)

Aldbrough Primary School, Aldbrough

Me And World Book Day

Dear Diary,
Today was World Book Day, I was feeling excited. I knew when I got to school everyone would be dressed up, what I didn't expect was all the teachers to have actually turned into their costumes. Mrs Gledden was the Hungry Caterpillar, she was so hungry that she started to eat my packed lunch, and Miss Harrison was a witch and turned Mr Brown into a frog. To stop the chaos, I locked them in the staff room. I ran home and hoped everything would be normal tomorrow, well, as normal as my school gets anyway!

Ariana Head (5)
Aldbrough Primary School, Aldbrough

The Kid Teacher

Dear Diary,

I've had a thought. Why can't kids run a school? I mean, we're taught by teachers every day, we are very sensible. So I'm going to kidnap the headteacher and take over the school! This is so awesome!

Two days later...

Okay, so I have managed to trick the other teachers into actually letting me do it, but right now in the story, I have the other kids constantly pestering me. How do the teachers deal? And to make matters worse, a kid spilt coffee down me. Total meltdown!

Isabelle Cooke (11)
Aldbrough Primary School, Aldbrough

Lucy's Magical Discovery

Dear Diary,

Today I went on a dog walk like usual, but this time we took a different pathway. But before we did, Nova and I heard a loud bang coming from the path we were going to walk through. Nova and I were really nervous and I'm only eleven years old, what was I going to do? At the time we were just standing there, until... we walked closer and closer. I started to see a bright, gloomy figure in the distance. I was amazed, the cutest little face stared up at me. Even Nova was surprised by it.

Kienna Leigh (10)

Aldbrough Primary School, Aldbrough

My New Family Day

This Wednesday morning, my dad said that I was going to a new house. I looked at my mum and was quite sad and excited because I was going to meet five brothers. I got put in the car, was driven to my new house and met my new brother called Tyke who was a dog. I had four cats too. I'd never seen them before and I liked chasing them. I had new bedding, a bowl and toys. I'm loved by my new family and I'm glad they picked me for my new adventure. Night everyone, excited for Thursday!

Liam Hodson (9)
Aldbrough Primary School, Aldbrough

Mer-Pup Friends

Dear Diary,

Yesterday was fun and also scary. First, I ate my breakfast and went outside. Secondly, I met my friends at Seaweed Cove Park, but... suddenly, a humongous shark swam at us. We all swam in different directions but the shark was swimming towards me. I hid in some seaweed and the shark went right next to me. Finally, it swam away. My friend Chloe and I swam to my house and ate a seaweed salad to calm down. After that, everyone went to have a good sleep.

Bella Stead (8)

Aldbrough Primary School, Aldbrough

The Life Of A Football

I'm awoken by grimy fingers squishing me, now I'm being booted out - children stepping, stabbing me. This Hadi guy who scares me recently fractured my forehead, and kicked Bob over three roofs! I'm booted into some bloke's hair. That hair's greasy. But worse: knobbly knees heading my way, *oof!* Sprained my nose! Heading towards some lunatics... phew, missed them. My vision is blurred... can't see anything, but feel wind on my face. Hit the roof, roll down, get bruised. *Boom! It's getting ridiculous!* Suddenly, *I'm so high up!* Those hard-hearted menaces aren't doing anything! Over the fence... I've landed. Peace.

Yusuf Zakariyya Ahsan (10)

Apex Primary School, Ilford

The Qur'an Competition

Dear Diary,

It was the day of the Qur'an competition. I was chosen from Year 3 to take part. I was starting to feel nervous with butterflies in my stomach. All the reciters were called one by one.

"Yaqoob Salahuddin," I heard and it was my turn now.

I confidently recited Surah An-Naba and then I spoke about its meanings without trembling. I heard an amazing recitation from KS3 and it was inspiring. Finally, it was time to announce the winners and I was determined to win.

As I waited anxiously, I heard, "Yaqoob Salahuddin."

My heart raced, I won!

Yaqoob Salahuddin (8)

Apex Primary School, Ilford

The Lion On Saturn

Last Saturday I wanted to explore. I got ready and looked through the telescope.

I saw my jet and I said, "I want to go to Saturn." It took me to Saturn. I saw a rainforest. I walked through, there was a lion! It was different shades of orange and surprisingly spoke to me in different languages. It started raining, the drops were rainbow-coloured. That's when I knew it made everything so colourful. We went into a cave, it was dark. We lit a lamp, there were lots of friendly animals, we played a game. Finally, it stopped raining.

Faatimah Hasan (7)

Apex Primary School, Ilford

The Time Yusuf Came

Dear Diary,

On Friday, after dinner, my mum said, "There will be a guest, and that guest will be Yusuf's dad."

So I asked, "Can Yusuf come too?"

And she said, "Okay, then I'll message his mum."

Then, after that, I played with my cousins. After about fifteen minutes, the doorbell rang so I went to open the door and it was him and his dad! So I asked him to come upstairs, then he came and we played on my cousin's PS4 and had a lot of fun. Then we all had to go back to our house.

Yusha Ali (9)

Apex Primary School, Ilford

Rose And The Mental Block

Dear Diary,

Today I woke up and then went on a glorious walk, but then I saw a beautiful landscape so I ran back home to get my paint kit. Then I returned back. I was about to paint it but I froze, it was like when I first painted, I had a mental block. I was so afraid for days and days, so afraid, I never painted for a very long time.

Just when things got dark, a spark came from the ground and said, "There's nothing to be scared of." Since then I never ever stopped painting again.

Izzah Usman (8)

Apex Primary School, Ilford

My Most Favourite And Exciting Day

On the 18th of December 2022, I woke up as usual along with my brother. We rushed downstairs to see if our parents were up. We were really surprised to see they were both ready and packed to go somewhere. We didn't know where! We all got in the car and my dad started driving. My brother and I were very eager to know where we were all headed. It took us both by surprise when the car stopped at the airport. In a heart-stopping moment, we were both stunned to find out that we were all going to Tenerife!

Haris Sufyan (9)
Apex Primary School, Ilford

Evil Dr iPad Comes Back

Today my mum asked me to go to the TV remote forest, I went with my big sister because there might be a stranger that is dangerous. Anyway, we were picking TV remotes but we saw... an iPad! We both knew Dr iPad was there! I ran back home but I saw that there was a party so I acted like a real TV, then mum muted me. I waited till the party was over. After I told mum, she called the FBI and doctors. The FBI arrested him. The doctors checked me and I malfunctioned. They fixed me.

Maryam Rono (8)
Apex Primary School, Ilford

A Surprise Visit To Legoland

I woke up and went to the kitchen and my mum told me that I was going to Legoland. I felt very shocked. But it was a school day. My mum told me that all my family was coming. It took a very long time to get there. We went on all the rides. The best ride was called Mythica, it was 3D and water went all over us. We had a family picnic and ate lots of lovely food. At the end, we took lots of pictures and I was able to buy a cool Lego set.

Humaira Adam (7)
Apex Primary School, Ilford

Superhero

Dear Diary,

My superhero saved the day. Ten people were stuck in a burning building and couldn't get out. My superhero flew in to save the day. A villain stopped me and kidnapped ten people and had taken them to an unknown location and I needed some backup and Super Sniffer the God Dog to sniff him out. We eventually found him in the sewers, he had an army and we had no choice but to fight his army. It was tough but we managed to beat them and saved the day and celebrated our victory.

Danny Murray-Starbuck (9)

Coastal Park School, Folkestone

Day Out

Dear Diary,

I went to London today, I was really excited. My mum, brothers, sister and I got on a train. We had to stay close to Mum as there were so many people. We all went on the London Eye, it was fun. We got food on the way home. I fell asleep on the train. We all had a really good day. Mum made us all popcorn and a hot drink and we all sat together and watched a film.

Ollie Wayland (8)
Coastal Park School, Folkestone

Ronaldo Versus Messi

Dear Diary,

Today I saw Ronaldo and Messi play against each other in a football match. The score was 5-4 to PSG, Messi's team. It was an amazing match, I had a fantastic time! After the match, I bought a Messi and Ronaldo shirt. Surprisingly, Ronaldo and Messi walked past me and I met them, I got a picture with them. It was the best time of my life.

Joseph (11)
Coastal Park School, Folkestone

Mum

Dear Diary,

I was at home and then I was in the car to get milk, but I wasn't coming back with the milk. There was no milk, that was why. I went home and played Fortnite, but first I gave Mum a hug from Fortnite.

Taylor Dunton (12)

Coastal Park School, Folkestone

The Monster In The Forest

Dear Diary,
I'll make it quick, these might be my final moments.
Today I was trudging through a dense forest like a
spidery tangle of trees, bushes and thorns. The
canopy was covered in a cloak of mist when I
came across a glow. I crept closer. Before me lay a
monster beyond your deepest, darkest nightmare,
with piercing blue eyes like bulging diamond balls.
Suddenly, it turned its head towards me. I ran for
my life, not daring to look back, and hid behind a
rock where I'm currently writing this. It's here!
Signing off,
Luke James Graham Porteous.

Luke Porteous (9)
Gayton CE Primary School, Gayton

The Flying School

Dear Diary,

Today I had a very horrendous day at school. Firstly, I was late for school. Secondly, I didn't complete my geography. Thirdly, at lunchtime, the school dramatically flew up to space and nearly hit an asteroid. And then it flew back down again and straight through the streets. And it also ran into a restraint and actually broke the restraint. We also flew halfway across the world, through India, Japan and also Russia. Fourthly, we landed safely on the ground. Finally, I got home from school and we lived happily ever after.

Jude Garfirth (9)

Gayton CE Primary School, Gayton

Super Soldier

Dear Diary,

I walked through time, feeling its thin line of generation at the bottom of my feet. Special moments such as the death of the dinosaurs, the discovery of the bulb and many more whizzed by me. Suddenly, it stopped. There was a crack on the fragile line. Icy cold water filled the tunnel. Who had done it? It was obviously a bullet. I stopped at 1940. I woke up to machine gun fire all around. Then I saw my enemy, General Katzenstein. I charged at him, blasting a jet of fire. *Bam!* Blackness.

Oliver Cooper (9)
Gayton CE Primary School, Gayton

Blood Dragon

Dear Diary,

I have had a really painful and surprising day, I just thought it would be a normal, bad day at school. I went to school and everything felt normal. First, I had horrible English and maths and after that it was break. But as soon as I got outside, I heard a huge flapping of giant wings. I slowly crept round to the corner of the wall and guess what I saw? I saw a huge, fire-breathing, blood-red dragon staring into my soul. Sweat meandered down my cheek. It reared up, this was it. The battle.

Ben Cooper (9)

Gayton CE Primary School, Gayton

The Super Snake

Dear Diary,

I had a rough day going from place to place. Not a lot of people were in the field, only me. Then, when it was about twenty minutes later, I saw some of my friends. I did not want to bother them, they might be having a marvellous time, so I kept on going because it was bedtime. I found a tunnel to stay in for the night. Then the morning came, it was raining heavily. Then I thought I found something to eat but then I thought I would make sure it lived a happy, wonderful life.

Lily Mussard (10)

Gayton CE Primary School, Gayton

The Worst Day Ever!

Dear Diary,

One morning I got out of my mum's bed way too late. I was too busy dreaming about being a steam train and puffing up my mouth. At eight o'clock I finally got up and realised that on my walk last night, when I was sliding on the road, I had hurt my paw! Then I rolled out of bed and hurt my ear! Then I ate my breakfast and tried to forget about it, even though I still had a burnt paw and a poorly ear. I still can't stop thinking about it, even a month later.

Macy Malyszewicz (8)

Gayton CE Primary School, Gayton

Journey Of A Lifetime

Dear Diary,

It was the best time of my life. I was captured and then had a battle with my trainer's enemy and friend and then he beat them. Secondly, we made a bond together and then we captured more together. Then we had an unstoppable team. We went to the Rock type gym and we needed Water type or Grass type and he used a Grass. Then we battled again and he won with a Grass type and I was weak against that type and we got the Rock badge. Then we went to get more creatures.

Dominic Mussard (8)

Gayton CE Primary School, Gayton

The Trip To New York

Dear Diary,

Today I woke up happily, ready to go to the busy airport to go on a holiday to New York City for Christmas. My family and I had to leave at half past six in the morning and the drive took one and a half hours. Once we got to the airport, we checked in but it took longer than we expected it to. Slowly, we went through security. After that, we went to the lounge and sat down, but then we had to move seats after we got on the plane and flew to New York.

Emily Mallalieu (9)

Gayton CE Primary School, Gayton

The Fight

Dear Diary,

Today at school it was hectic. I got into a fight with my friend! First, we were just in magic class until we got called up to perform a simple spell we learnt as it was the end of the semester. So, I started to think about which spell to use. *Hmm.* I finally picked one and we started. He shouted his spell at me and I blocked, but when I tried, he shot the best spell they knew at me. I was hit. I got knocked out for ages. *Ugh!*

Athena Smith (9)

Gayton CE Primary School, Gayton

Garfield

Dear Diary,

A few days ago, I was eating whatever I saw and sat down to have a nap. But when I woke up, my house was empty and guess who had moved in? My biggest hater, the cutest cat in the world. But I had just realised that I was dreaming, then I woke up and I was fine. Then I went upstairs for a nap and then slept for the last hours of the day. It was time for dinner for me which was Vito's pizza.

Ollie Boardman (9)
Gayton CE Primary School, Gayton

A Dragon Destroys The City

Dear Diary,

I woke up and went downstairs to get breakfast and I saw a diabolical dragon and it tried to destroy our city. I had to fight it. Now my body was full of bruises, it hurt really badly. He could breathe fireballs and out of his nose he shot fire and it flew really fast. When it flew I shot it and boom! The ground shook as the dragon landed against the ground. Then the day was normal.

Sonny Fitzgerald (9)

Gayton CE Primary School, Gayton

Deku's Diary

Dear Diary,

Today was awful, we went to a training gym and one of our teachers almost died by using her Quirk trying to save us, but the bad guys made us spread out to different parts of the gym and I got teleported to the water part and I punched the water to make a strategy. Then we got to the boss and I saved one of our teachers, but we still ended up in hospital.

Jack Wade (10)

Gayton CE Primary School, Gayton

JD's Fantastic Adventures

Dear Diary,

Today was great. It was a wonderful day at the Jurassic Coast and suddenly, as I was mining away with my hammer and chisel, I found a tooth. It was a brachiosaur tooth. I chipped some more. I found a whole skull. I reported it to a museum nearby and they said that they would pay me one million for it. As I had a lot of money, I donated it all to charity.

Alex Beresford Linnell (10)

Gayton CE Primary School, Gayton

A Mythical Battle

Dear Diary,

I had a tough day. I had to fight a mythical creature, and when I was fighting it I sneaked up on it and jumped on him and then I fell and the monster spotted me. But I didn't tell you I made a trap and I led him in it, but he jumped out so my friend Jake distracted him, came on and ran with me so he would get stuck.

Sean Holligan (7)

Gayton CE Primary School, Gayton

Diary Of A Wimpy Kid

Dear Diary,

Today I woke up to my brother, Rodrick, rapidly waving my blanket, letting in all the cold air. Under the blanket, my legs were cold and hairs on end. Today is hopefully going to be better. I know yesterday I was late for the bus but I need to be on time, so I don't miss my English test and fail.

Summer Maddocks (10)

Gayton CE Primary School, Gayton

The Alien Came To The Planet

Dear Diary,

Once there was a calm city but an alien wanted to destroy the planet. All the villagers were scared. The alien tried to kill the villagers who ran for their lives.

"Eek! Help! Help!"

The alien was tough and green. Some people hid in their houses, safe.

"Hahaha!"

Happy and safe and sound, while the others fought hard, tough and strong. The alien was brave and tough, but feeling scared that he wasn't going to win the tough fight while the villagers fought roughly and strongly. The alien was really tough and hard.

"I believe in myself."

Arthur Hobkinson (6)

Grampound Road Village CE School, Truro

Larry The Book Eater

"Wow," everyone says about Larry when Larry goes to school.

Every time Larry goes to school and finishes his test, his teacher gets amazed. When he can, he eats a few books, but he's always wondered what other food tastes like. The next day, he started to feel sick and thought it was because he had eaten too many books, so he thought to try some bread which wasn't too bad. He thought to himself, *I should keep eating different things.*

The next day, on the news it said, "The boy who eats lots of books has eaten food finally."

George Walker (10)

Grampound Road Village CE School, Truro

A Day Of Hatred!

I was euphoric because it's my favourite day of the year (besides Annual Skincare Day), Valentine's Day. I don't need to think twice about who'd be my Valentine, it's definitely my best friend, Agatha. We've been each other's Valentines since we were children and both Agatha and I would definitely stay true to this tradition. So I just dropped my note off and saw Agatha give hers to her husband, Jedros. I felt a burst of fury bubble inside me and before I knew it, my finger was glowing with magic and I shot Agatha with a burst of fire!

Lilly Grace Johns (9)

Grampound Road Village CE School, Truro

Pokémon Master Journeys

Today I have been battling Charizard. We tried to defeat them but we couldn't take him out so I returned Gengar for Chinchou and we defeated Leon and Charizard. So then the journeys continued, then I found Eevee and had a party with food and drinks. All of my friends came over to the party. Team Rocket came with Meowth and Wobbuffet, then they made sure that no one was there and there were no people there. So they crashed the party and went back to their base and got another Pokémon, Grookey, and distracted everyone until the journeys continued...

Miles Purshouse (9)
Grampound Road Village CE School, Truro

The Disastrous School

Dear Diary,

It's me, and I am called Milly, this diary is all about my school. In school, there is a rude girl called Jasmine and there's also a nice boy called Max. Last week at school, Jasmine said that I was fat and ugly. She has always been a bully to me, it has been from Year 1 to Year 6.

So yesterday I told her to, "Stop being a bully."

And she replied, "Me, a bully?"

"Yes, you."

And so she said back, "Okay, I promise I will stop if you forgive me."

So I kindly forgave her.

Macey Knowles (8)

Grampound Road Village CE School, Truro

Under The Sea

Dear Diary,

My best bud (Lewis) and I were just wandering around when we saw some yummy, juicy fish. We dived into the sea and started eating. After a while, we got so full we decided to go back to land, but we didn't see what was coming... *A giant polar bear* was standing right there, waiting. We tried to escape but we were too slow. Luckily we had a polar bear friend who told the other polar bear to stop.

Our friend said, "Be careful next time."

Lewis and I nodded our heads. Now we are so careful.

Lily-Sue Moran (11)

Grampound Road Village CE School, Truro

The Adventures Of Magu And Coco

Magu woke up next to a giant orb and then he decided to touch it. As soon as his arm came into contact with the orb, he immediately felt energised and he saw a portal near a collapsed structure. He decided to enter it and he teleported next to a giant tree!

"This place is weird," muttered Magu while exploring.

He decided to get some coconuts to eat.

As soon as he started to eat one, he heard, "Ow!" from the coconut, and then legs sprouted out of the coconut, then a head, and it introduced itself as Coco.

Connor Ryan (8)

Grampound Road Village CE School, Truro

A Diary Of Lucy In Narnia

Dear Diary,

We were sailing towards an unknown island on the Dawn Treader. We got onto the sailboats and started rowing towards land. As we neared the island, we could see it was as silent as the dead. Soon after, we docked the boats and started to search the island. It was barren; desolate, we couldn't find a single soul in sight. In the middle of the quiet city, there was a church; on the church was a tall church spire with a clock in it. Then, we slowly opened the door into the grasp of the icy cold darkness...

Amelia Jones (10)
Grampound Road Village CE School, Truro

Careful What You Read Before Bed

Dear Diary,

So I was in bed after saying night to my family and I dreamt off to sleep. When I woke up, I put on my school uniform and headed out the door. Then the weirdest thing happened, I was stuck in the dark woods, alone and terrified.

I started walking to school but then I heard a growl and a deep voice, "What are you doing in my woods?"

I turned and ran towards school, opened the door and fell through. I opened my eyes and found the Gruffalo book next to me. It was all a dream!

Madeleine Everton (6)

Grampound Road Village CE School, Truro

Imagine Kitticorns!

Dear Diary,

Once upon a time, a long time ago, there were cats all around the world in places called Europe and Asia. Europe is where we live now! Kitticorns are very rare things and they are almost extinct but some still live. Girls and boys, if you have nightmares then kitticorns will find you good things, and if kitticorns don't come, that means you are a naughty girl or a naughty boy. A kitticorn's favourite colour is rainbow and kitticorns come in all types like kittipets and kitticats!

Amelia Hill (6)

Grampound Road Village CE School, Truro

My Unicorn Day

Dear Diary,

Today I was turned into a unicorn by an evil witch, and after she turned me into a unicorn she put me in a zoo, and no animal wants to be in a zoo. As you all know, unicorns have magic powers, so I used those magic powers to blast the zoo gates open. *Bam!* The gates exploded, so I ran out of the shattered gates and ran to the witch's cottage. The witch was tending to her beloved roses, and with my magic powers, I blasted her into bits and the spell was reversed.

Florence Smith-Allen (10)

Grampound Road Village CE School, Truro

The Octopus That Talks To A Human

Dear Diary,

Hi there, you're probably wondering what I am and what my name is. Well, my name is Ben and I am an octopus. And you might be really confused by how I can talk, it might be your imagination. But yes, what it really is, well, the secret is magic dust. Do you want to know where you can get it? You can get it from a magical fairy or you could get it from a magical elf that has a superpower but never realises it because the elf is too scared and frightened to use it.

Evie Clifford (7)

Grampound Road Village CE School, Truro

The Happy Pirate Diary

I once had a beautiful wooden ship called the Pelican with sharp points. One day, piece by piece, Pelican fell to pieces and into the cold sea and nothing but water rushed past me. After, I had to build it back together with glue but we had to get it from the shop. When I got back, three people were robbing my ship. I fought with a cutlass and one of them fell off the ship into the shivering sea. Then I sailed the seven seas to the sunset and lived happily ever after on the Pelican.

Oliver Keaveney (6)

Grampound Road Village CE School, Truro

Best Friends Forever

At school today I made a new friend, he was called Bluey. We played tag and hide-and-seek. We had pizza for lunch. I love eating food. After lunch we did maths and we sat next to each other. After school, we went to the park and we played on the swings and the slide and the monkey bars. After the park, we went to Bluey's house for tea. We had fish and chips and ice cream for pudding. Meeting Bluey today has made me feel very happy. I am so glad I went to school today, thank you.

Grace Purshouse (5)

Grampound Road Village CE School, Truro

Bob's Quest

My name is Bob. My tribe sent me to kill the Devil and the heir to his throne, Michael. On my quest to succeed, the King gave me the Sword of the Ultimate Fire Griffin. Now if I failed, the planet would die from the Devil. So off I went, heading to the Devil's Den, when my ship landed in a pool of acid. I had to eject otherwise I would be dissolved by acid. When I met the Devil eye to eye, I stabbed him in the chest with the sword. I then realised the Devil was my father!

Tom Milburn (10)

Grampound Road Village CE School, Truro

Fishermen Escape

Dear Diary,

Yesterday I was swimming away from the evil fishermen. They were trying to catch me with their net, I felt scared. I swam and I jumped away from their hook. Then I noticed a fast, red fish. I followed it as the fishermen chased me and it led me to some golden armour! I put it on and a fishing hook hit me.

I said, "Phew, that was lucky!"

I batted the hook back with my tail and it tied the fishermen up.

Thomas Kinsey-Jones (7)
Grampound Road Village CE School, Truro

The Runaway Doughnuts

Dear Diary,

It was a lovely day at the local bakery until I got a really disturbing call that said that all bakery doughnuts had to be eaten in... one... two... three... four... *wait... four weeks?* I had over 300 doughnuts to sell though! Never mind. But oh no! My doughnuts were on the loose! I'd have to call Alyssa's doughnut rescue.

"Hello!"

"Hello, how can I help?"

"All my bakery doughnuts are on the loose!"

"Okay, well we will send me and my crew up to help."

And that is how Alyssa and her crew saved the day!

Alyssa Graham (9)

Grange Park Primary School, Sunderland

Burrito's Big Adventure

Dear Diary,

Burrito's friend, Bean, went missing. Burrito searched for hours trying to find Bean. He eventually called his other friend, Hotdog, but even with both of them looking they still couldn't find him. But the next day, Burrito came home and told Bean's wife her husband was missing and she freaked out. All four of them searched and weeks passed, they nearly gave up, but they didn't check Bean's favourite place, the bowling alley. But he wasn't there. Next, the owner of the alley had said that Bean might be locked up at evil Broccoli's. They might find Bean...

Lucas Bramley (9)

Grange Park Primary School, Sunderland

Adventure Of Pokémon: Galar Region

Dear Diary,

In the Galar region, there was a Pokémon trainer. For his starter he chose Grookey. His name was Isaac. He went into the forest, he met a Pokémon with a sword in its mouth, it was called Zacian. Nothing worked to attack it so he ran away. He ended up becoming Champion. He went to a place called the Isle of Armor, he caught Squirtle. After, he went to the Crown Tundra. He caught three legendary birds, Zapdos, Moltres and Articuno. He caught five Regis, Registeel, Regirock, Regice and Regidrago. He travelled the world. He became Champion everywhere!

Isaac Hill (8)

Grange Park Primary School, Sunderland

Angel And Stitch

A long time ago, Angel was in school and there was a new student coming in. The teacher sent him in and he was very shy.

The teacher said, "What's your favourite colour?"

He said, "Blue."

Emma said, "He is mine."

And the boy said, "My name is Stitch."

Then Stitch was in love. He asked Angel out.

She said, "*No!*"

Then she ran behind the door.

She really liked him so she ran back and said, "I like you. Oops. I was not supposed to say that!"

Then they fell in love.

Esme McGhee (9)
Grange Park Primary School, Sunderland

The Incredible Diary Of Captain Underpants

Dear Diary,

There was a principal. Then a boy called Harold. He used a Hypno Ring and turned the principal into Captain Underpants. Meanwhile, a scientist found a sign that said: *Need A Science Teacher*. His name was Professor Poopypants. After he built a massive toilet robot, Captain Underpants used one fist and it crumbled straight away, but some androids defeated him. He was outnumbered but he got lots of power. He did a mega punch and destroyed all of the androids, but there was one left. He used a powerful mega punch and defeated it. Then he got wet.

Freddie Harrison (8)

Grange Park Primary School, Sunderland

The Day Of Jury

Dear Diary,

I found my missing friend. I was called to go to the jury to find out who killed my friend, Chop Chop. The judge was very mad, the wolf was very scary with big, red eyes and raging, sharp claws.

He said, "I'm not guilty. I was getting some cake ingredients for my sick gran."

He wanted sugar so he went to Chop's house and he huffed and puffed and blew Chop's house down.

I said, "I think he's guilty."

The judge said, "The fox is not guilty. We are giving him a cake and one pound."

Isabella Hill-Collings (9)

Grange Park Primary School, Sunderland

The Guy Who Gets An Autograph

Dear Diary,
Someone went to a concert and they became friends and watched the show together. After that, they went and got some ice cream together and went back to watch the show and ended up at the front of the stage and then some breakdancers came out. Once the dance finished, the singing people came out and sang the best song. Finally, George got the autograph, the thing that he'd been wanting for two hours, and guess what? He got the autograph from his favourite breakdancer and the two of them were excited and went home happy and excited.

Thomas Raine-Dent (8)

Grange Park Primary School, Sunderland

WWII

Dear Diary,
In France, I was battling the German army when my rifle jammed. I had to take my dead friend's rifle and we were under heavy machine gun fire. We pushed the Germans and captured their weapons. Adolf Hitler wasn't happy about that, so he sent more troops and they took us to Poland. We eventually escaped, but they got us again and they kept us in Poland to work in the fields. We looked for the Germans for five years. These are the names of my friends: Pete, Freddie, Trevor, Kieran, Sam, Tom, Ollie, Logan, Oliver and Leo.

JJ Broome (9)
Grange Park Primary School, Sunderland

Jurassic Park At Court

Dear Diary,

I went to court and I didn't know why. I found out sooner rather than later, and the reason was... two-thirds of the pigs were killed by the Big Bad Wolf. I knew my pet baby triceratops didn't know what was going on.

I did know and I thought the wolf was guilty, but his story was, "I had the flu so I sneezed one and two's houses down."

But I didn't believe him. He apparently was making a cake for his grandmother and all he needed was sugar, but his list needed sugar and a birthday card...

Oliver Bussell (8)

Grange Park Primary School, Sunderland

Secret Kingdom Phoenix Festival Guide

"I don't think I could be wearing any more clothes!" Esmae giggled to her best friends Rubie and Summer.

Ruby was wearing a long dress with tights and a woolly hoodie. Summer was wearing a short woolly coat with a big shirt on, with big pants that had love hearts on them. When they were at the festival, they found Summer's dad handing out sparklers. Summer, Esmae and Rubie all got two sparklers and put the sparklers in a big tub. Next to the tub was a hotdog stand. After they put their sparklers in the tub, they ate.

Summer Daley (8)
Grange Park Primary School, Sunderland

The Day My Teammate Got Injured

Dear Diary,

I was driving to the Sunderland stadium and we got the lineup. We walked onto the pitch but it was a final and if we lost we would be out. The whistle blew, it was Bristol City versus Sunderland. Ross Stewart passed the ball to Roberts, he ran up and the next thing we saw was a goal. 1-0 to Sunderland. Bristol City were annoyed. He ran up the line and passed it to Clarke. He defended it and slide-tackled! He twisted his ankle, they got into a fight. The referee gave them a penalty. They scored! Yes!

Jayden Prescott (9)

Grange Park Primary School, Sunderland

I Win

One Saturday, I was playing a football match with my football team against another team. We kicked off and I scored a left-footed goal. My team scored four more goals, the other team scored one goal and a penalty. Sadly, I had an injury and bruised my big toe. I came back on the pitch. Eventually, the match ended and after that, I got McDonald's for dinner, went on my Xbox for one hour and then I had a nice, warm bath. I watched my favourite TV show and went to my nana's house and I had sausage and mash.

Jake Broomfield (9)
Grange Park Primary School, Sunderland

Leo's Diary

Hello, this is my diary, I will tell you all my events now. I am dating my one-year crush, I will update you later. Day two. You will never guess what, I had my first kiss, bye. I really like Spider-Man, also I play video games, they are my favourite. I have literally just caught Flareon in Pokémon *but! I have a Rhyperior and it is better!* I have 100 skins or over on a video game. I had a really good victory as well. I have seven crown wins and that equals first wins. Sorry, I am not bragging.

Leo Davidson (9)
Grange Park Primary School, Sunderland

Winning The Lottery

Have you ever wondered what you'd do if you won the lottery? My mum won, she did, really. Okay, she didn't win the jackpot, we don't live in a great big mansion. I wouldn't want to, even if Mum had won mega millions, I'd hate to live in a big house. If I ever lived in a big house I would want the smallest room because I don't want a big room, because loads of things would get messy and every day I would have to clean my room. But with a small room, it wouldn't get as messy then.

Sadie Stubbs (9)

Grange Park Primary School, Sunderland

The Girl Who Entered A Fashion Show

Dear Diary,

A girl was homeless and was walking the street, then she saw a fashion show that said whoever won would get a diamond dress. Her name was Jessica, she wanted to get that dress so she entered herself in, then she went back to her hut and got her money jar and got £3.30 and went back and there were about 100 people there. Then she got called out and she won. She was so happy, then they gave her £5000 and when she left she bought a house and had a baby that was a girl.

Kayci Preen (9)

Grange Park Primary School, Sunderland

Little Pig And The Bad Wolf

One day, I lost my little pig in the forest and the pigs built three houses: one straw, one brick and one metal. The Big Bad Wolf had to sneak and tried not to sneeze but he huffed and puffed and the wolf sneezed and blew it down. The wolf had a cold. He went to the pharmacy and bought medicine for his cold. It was his old grandmother's birthday and he wanted to bake a cake for her. He got flour and butter but the wolf forgot the birthday card, but finally, he got the card.

Evie Playle (8)
Grange Park Primary School, Sunderland

The Incredible Diary Of A Cat

There once was a cat named Milo, Milo was nice and sweet. One day, Milo fell off a tree branch and got badly hurt. He was sitting in a pile of leaves, trying to recover. He sat there really sad because he had no family members to go to. One day he got found and put up for adoption. He waited days and days and days until a lovely family came and adopted him. They had a cat tree, cat bowls, cat toys and cat treats and they lived happily ever after in the house full of cat toys.

Lilah Mae Downing (8)

Grange Park Primary School, Sunderland

The Incredible Diary Of Lexi

Dear Diary,

My owner had left for school and I was really bored and my name is Lexi. I thought that I could go to the beach and play in the park so I went and crawled through the fence and went to the beach. It was really hot. Everyone had ice cream and fish and chips. I wanted some really bad. I saw some in a bag. I ran and ran till I was there. I saw the birds looking for food. I ate it fast because they wanted it. It was mine, not their food!

Lacey Maw (9)

Grange Park Primary School, Sunderland

The Robot

A robot got arrested and got a vote. He did not get arrested but he killed two little sheep and blew their house down and one sheep was still alive in the city centre. Because he was not guilty, he got cake. On the list were flour, eggs, sugar and milk. And he had a bag to do the list. He killed the two sheep because he had a very bad cold. The city centre was at the back of Boots. He went to his gran to make a cake with the things on the list.

Elliott Potts (9)

Grange Park Primary School, Sunderland

Awakening From The Curse: Revenge At Last!

Dear Diary,

A thousand years have passed since Sorceress Elena cursed me and Ollie. Many things have changed, for instance, there is a strange moving wheelbarrow called a *car*. There's a moving mirror called a television. How strange! But Ollie and I will not let anything hold us back! We have been fish for the last thousand years. Now to commence our original plan: *take over the world*. I suppose it's a good thing that we're forgotten, it'll surprise everyone who thinks we're long gone! But I don't know why we're forgotten. After all, we were infamous!

By Veronica.

Maariyah Jiwani (11)
Noor Ul Islam Primary School, Leyton

The Diary Of The Acer Laptop

Dear Diary,

I am a lonely Acer laptop. I used to have a friend, a girl called Nusaibah Mirza, who nicknamed me Pace. She's a very nice girl who called me a friend. Today I became unwell and my power button stopped working. Now I lie in this lonely drawer under Nusaibah's brother's bed, dreading the day that he will come and take all my screws out. It's a dreadful thing that humans call 'taking apart'. I do try to make friends but the screwdrivers bully me and call me 'human's pet'. And if the screwdrivers say something, everyone does.

Nusaibah Mirza (10)
Noor Ul Islam Primary School, Leyton

My Heart Has Shattered Like Glass

Dear Diary,

Father will forever be engraved in my heart. Everyone cherishes his loss and wishes him a peaceful sleep. Mother says not to be dismal but how can't I? My best friend has just died. It all happened in a rush. I lay awake from a roll of thunder.

But, people say, "You shouldn't live in the past."

I can do nothing to bring him back. All I can say is this accursed plague is controlling our fates. As I walked home, I felt the plague mocking my fears. The bomb of reality has hit me. Good night. Susannah.

Maryam Imran (11)

Noor Ul Islam Primary School, Leyton

Dreamland Diary

Dear Diary,

My name is Rahmah, and today I discovered that I have a superpower! A superpower that grants me the ability to travel the universe! I first floated off into my very own cotton candy land. Oh, how fluffy it felt! I had my very own cotton candy palace to myself. I saw, just then, a cotton candy rocket. I jumped in and zoomed away into a marshmallow mansion. I took a bite into that luscious, chewy wall of wonder and felt myself moving again, off to another dream. I awoke in bed.

Would I visit the land again?

Rahmah Salahuddin (11)

Noor Ul Islam Primary School, Leyton

The Mysterious Discovery

Dear Diary,

My name is Ayesha and I am ten. I am in a place called Sweetville. It all started after school, when I saw an enormous gem stuck on my wardrobe. I was so curious that I pushed it and found myself in this yummy world, but I realised that I couldn't go home. Luckily, I met a friend named Lucy and she told me that the only way I could return home was to obtain the sparkling emerald. It sounded easy, until Lucy told me that we had to find it before an evil person called Shuriki...

Ayesha Saeed (10)

Noor Ul Islam Primary School, Leyton

The Stalkers

The sun disappeared behind the pointed silhouettes of the rooftops of Strawtree Town. A thick, eerie darkness fell like no other night Strawtree had ever known. The moon itself barely had enough courage to peek around the clouds, as though it knew that tonight something strange was going to happen. Mothers and fathers of Strawtree would usually tuck their children into bed, but what they didn't know was that tonight could be the last night for their children. Midnight. One o'clock. Two o'clock. *Creak!* A strange noise broke the silence. *Creak!* Lucy's mum and dad were gone. Lucy was petrified.

Nancy-Ann Jackson (10)
Roydon Primary School, Roydon

What To Do When You've Changed The World

Okay, what have I done? Discovered that one of the largest urban legends is true? Maybe. Ever heard of the story of Atlantis? Not just a myth, apparently. Imagine this, you're scuba diving for the first time, and you hear a clink and spot dust spinning around you in the ocean. Yep, Atlantis. For the next six hours, interviews, newspapers, and even sponsors. Fun fact: being world famous isn't fun. Very tiring. But woah! That's not something you do every day. Surprised nobody found it sooner. Hailey Brooks, the kid who proved a myth. By accident, of course. What else?

Grace Pearce (11)
Roydon Primary School, Roydon

Matilda And The Mysterious Rabbits

Dear Diary,

Today Matilda went to the pet shop and got five rabbits. She named them Peter, Benjamin, Flopsy, Mopsy and Cottontail. They looked just like ordinary rabbits, thought Matilda. She took them home and put them in a nice, cosy cage. Matilda did the usual stuff you'd do, like feed them and play with them. One ordinary day, Matilda took the rabbits out of their cage. She felt so surprised. Her rabbits could talk. They had lots of chats in coffee shops and were very happy indeed. They played and played and went to bed happily, dreamily and sleepily.

Isla Betts (8)

Roydon Primary School, Roydon

Skye's Magical Journey

Dear Diary,

My little friend is a capybara, her name is Skye. She is small, fluffy and friendly. Skye went for a walk and found a forest, a very magical place. Skye was scared, lost and crying. A little white, furry bunny appeared and asked what was wrong. Skye told her that she was lost and her human friend would worry about her.

Bunny said, "Don't be afraid, I know how to get you home. First, let's go have some fun. My friends are waiting for me at the rainbow river."

They had fun, then it was time for home.

Lexie Edgar-Ayms (8)
Roydon Primary School, Roydon

When The Boba And Coffee Disappeared

Dear Diary,

I was on my way to Hawaii on a plane to explore different things. Then I went to get off the plane and ran straight to the boba tea shop and bought one and guess what happened? I made a friend. He was really nice. He decided to buy a coffee. That was when it first started. The coffee and boba tea fell in love.

Suddenly the coffee fell out of his hands. *Crash!* He was broken. As soon as he fell the boba tea fell too.

"Wow, our drinks are gone!"

"I know, what a shame."

Scarlett Apea-Agyei (8)
Roydon Primary School, Roydon

Earthquake: 6th Of February

Dear Diary,

It all happened so suddenly whilst I was asleep. The house shook so aggressively that it woke me up. My whole body was trembling with fear, I had goosebumps all over me. I could hear people screaming and shouting. The walls started to crack and the ceiling started to cave in. Quickly I leapt out of bed and dashed for the door, grabbing hold of my baby brother. I got out onto the landing just as my mum and dad appeared. I looked at them for reassurance but they just looked frightened. We needed to get out...

Emily Skulski (10)
Roydon Primary School, Roydon

Bella Bunny

Hello, last year we went on holiday to the UK. We had lots of fun until we found something *very* strange in the bushes. We saw a bunny. We picked her up and named her Bella... Bella Bunny. We took her home and then we became best friends. Until one day I woke up and found she was missing, so I cried my eyes out and told my mum. She told me, "Look properly."

I just went upstairs and cried, like really cried. I started to throw my pillows at the wall and there I saw my Bella Bunny. *Wow!*

Abrianna Asiamah (9)
Roydon Primary School, Roydon

Diary Of A Disastrous Dog

We were at home. My family always thinks I'm a disaster, they won't take me anywhere. But as they'd signed me up for a swim club, I could go crazy. Tuesday. I was at home, scratching my owner's boy to get all the food I wanted, I was so excited. I did some droppings in the house (hehe). I got shouted at but still could go swimming. When we got there, I did a front flip, I wasn't meant to do one. I put red dye in the pool but suddenly found myself at home getting told off. Worth it!

Emiah Cull (9)

Roydon Primary School, Roydon

A Day In The Life Of Fish Face

Dear Diary,

Today, I started like I normally do by heading downstairs and getting some fish flakes and pellets. So I poured it into my bowl and ate it. After that, with my awesome fish hearing I heard my mum shout that I had to get dressed because I forgot it was fish school today. I rushed upstairs and got dressed, but when I looked at the time I was late! I ran as fast as I possibly could to tell my mum what time it was, but after all of that, it was too late.

Signing off,

Fish Face.

Joe Armitt (9)

Roydon Primary School, Roydon

The Bean That Travelled The World

Dear Diary,

Today I went on a plane to Hawaii! I arrived at 3:30 so I went to get some amazing dinner. My next stop will be NYC, very excited!

When I woke up, I went on a train. All the seats were taken so I sat on the floor. I got to the airport and hopped on my plane.

Today I arrived at 6:32 so again I got some dinner. I had pizza today, *yummy!* It was 10/10. I went to my modern hotel room. NYC is beautiful. This trip has been so fun!

Diary written by Bean,
Adios!

Lexi Bond (9)
Roydon Primary School, Roydon

Cupid And Tammy Looking For An Adventure

Dear Diary,

Today we escaped and we had an adventure. We were going to sneakily roll away and sneak into her car. She was going to the airport so we hid under her seat. Finally, we landed in... France? I was shocked, Tammy said so too. We rolled our way to eat and then went to Paris. We also saw the Eiffel Tower, it was way too cold and way too big. She started taking selfies near it with her lips stuck out like a duck. And at the end, we sat under a bench and also ate our lunch.

Nicole Nikalova (9)
Roydon Primary School, Roydon

Trapped

Dear Diary,

I was in a nightmare. I was in the dark and I could not get out. I was trapped but there was something there, something that was invisible. It made a noise, a creepy noise. I was so scared, I wanted to get out of this nightmare but there was no way out. I was not going anywhere. There were no doors, no windows, nothing, it was just me and that noise. But then there was just a minute of silence, then I heard my mum and dad. I was starting to wake up. It was over.

Poppy Wilkinson
Roydon Primary School, Roydon

The Day I Went Back

I was in my chair, waiting for something fun to happen outside, when a rift opened up in the sky and sucked me in. I was confused but scared at the same time, and when I opened my eyes again I was laying on a rock in front of a huge, scary T-rex. I got up hastily and got out of there. I was in the Jurassic period. *How did I get here?* I thought as I wandered around, looking for some food. I found some berries and I had no choice but to eat them. Let's hope I survive.

Harry Fairweather (11)
Roydon Primary School, Roydon

Family Days

On Friday, my baby cousin and I went for a walk past the park. We found some cats. Lola, my cousin, was so excited, she wanted to touch the cats but they kept running away. She started to cry but then the cats came back. She stopped crying because she was happy to see them, but then it started to rain so we all ran back home. But the good thing was that we had a nice, hot roast dinner waiting for us that Nanny had cooked. We all sat down and started to eat. We had a lovely day.

Ruby-Mae Tennens (9)
Roydon Primary School, Roydon

A Day In The Life Of A Koala And Sloth

Dear Diary,

Today my BFF (Koazy the koala) and I got to meet up and have lots of fun. First, we went to Fairytale Land, then we went to Cloud Coffee Shop. Then we looked at the time and it was only 1pm so we then went to the cafe and both got two fluffaccinos and a waffle each. Then we decided to go shopping to decorate our rooms and we found fluffy stools, pillows and cute posters. Then we spent the night looking at the sunset. BFFs forever, fluffaccinos forever!

Roxy Martin (9)
Roydon Primary School, Roydon

Diary Of A Wimpy Kid

Today, my best friend Rowley and I were at school. It was all good until we were having lunch, we were just talking. Rowley said he had a new best friend. This made me very jealous, his new best friend was his next-door neighbour. I was walking home today and I saw Rowley and his new neighbour in his garden. I asked if I could join in and we all became friends.

Sophie Haddrick (8)
Roydon Primary School, Roydon

Time Travel Adventures!

One red-haired dog and a red-head girl travel backwards and forwards in a time portal whirl. Exploring together, a world of snow where nothing but unusual mammals did grow, the wonders of the Ice Age, you know! No shoes needed living in the wilderness outside, the Stone Age is my kind of crazy life! Whoa, spinning forwards we go, so much to explore that we don't already know! Bring back treasures, all kinds of silver, gold and pearls. Experiment! Experiment! Never doubt that a small group of concerned people can change this world. Bye for now, Diary,

Izzwizz and Scouty-Boo!

Izabella Salisbury (9)

Ryhall CE Academy, Ryhall

17th February 2023

Dear Diary,

Today was the worst day of my life. It all started off when the teacher said we'd be performing a musical in front of the entire school and everyone had a speaking part. About five seconds later, I started to feel sweatiness and tingling in my hands. *I was having a panic attack!* I tried to do deep breaths but it didn't change anything. I started fiddling with my fingers which helped a little.

I eventually said to myself, "What's the worst that could happen? It's not going to kill me," and I started to feel better.

Anonymous (9)

Ryhall CE Academy, Ryhall

The Diary Of Captain Firebeard

Dear Diary,

Yesterday, me and me crew found the magical treasure of Captain Ludo. I was so excited to get me hands on the mythical lightning sword. The glow of the blade could be seen from miles away, which attracted the scurvy crew of the Jenga ship. They thought they could steal me treasure? Think again, for I am Captain Firebeard! So I held me mighty lightning sword and electrocuted the enemy. After that, we looted their ship and set sail for home. Little did we know, the Kraken was waiting.

So I told the crew, "We're having calamari tonight!"

Rudy Maltby (9)
Ryhall CE Academy, Ryhall

Jake The Incredible Explorer

Dear Diary,

Yesterday I was walking through the green, wild jungle and I got chased by a wolf. I ran as fast as I could towards a cold, blue waterfall. Leading from the waterfall was a beautiful, blue river. In the river, there were peculiar, pink dolphins with bright, orange stars on their backs and rainbows as eyebrows. Then I looked up and saw a bright, gold monkey eating his yummy, yellow bananas. We laughed and played rock, paper, scissors for a while and shared another banana, then I woke up and thought that was fun, but only a dream.

Jacob Allwright (9)

Ryhall CE Academy, Ryhall

Day In Disney

Dear Diary,

Yesterday, I went to Disney World Orlando to visit Animal Kingdom and I went to watch the Lion King show. I felt really excited. My family and I were watching the performers on the trapeze, they were flying through the air freely, with big smiles on their bright faces. The singers were very confident and they were singing loud and clear. Then, all of a sudden, they called me out from the audience and helped me onto the trapeze. I was exhilarated and I felt free, as the wind blew through my hair. It was a delightful experience.

Orlaith Heames (9)

Ryhall CE Academy, Ryhall

Bailey The Super Dog

Dear Diary,
One morning I woke up from an amazing dream, it was marvellous. Mummy and my sisters left for school and work. Finally, I was all alone in the house. I had a funny feeling, it was like I had superpowers. I walked over to the washing, I suddenly started ironing. I thought it was a dream, but it wasn't. I was actually doing it. After ironing, I washed up. Even though I didn't like my paws wet. Suddenly I started to cook. I finally finished just in time as Mummy and my sisters came home.
Bailey the Dog.

Lilly-Ella Veasey (9)
Ryhall CE Academy, Ryhall

Kiki And The Forest Fire!

Today, whilst perched on my favourite eucalyptus tree, I became aware of a funny smell. I heard a noise overhead and looked up to see birds flying away from the forest. In the distance, smoke was seeping through the trees. Instantly, I saw flames bursting through the trees. It was petrifying. I climbed down the tree and scurried away as quickly as I could. I could feel the heat of the fire and there were flames all around me. Just when I thought the flames would catch me, hands reached towards me and lifted me up. I was safe again.

Ava Lidgley (9)
Ryhall CE Academy, Ryhall

Frank's Story

It was June 1944. Frank was only seventeen years old when he joined the RAF. He left his family and friends behind and lied about his age, he wanted to fight for his country. Despite his young age, he proved to be brave, strong, smart and bold. He made many friends and he lost many. One day, a horrible accident happened and Frank was injured. Rescued by the other pilot, he survived but lost his leg. He couldn't fly again but he became the greatest teacher of all to the many young pilots. He was ninety-six years old this month.

Winston Lambert (8)
Ryhall CE Academy, Ryhall

A Day In The Life Of Robert Smith, Soldier In World War I

Dear Diary,

I am writing this from a poppy field in France, it is 26th February 1917. My past few days have been terrible, well, even worse. It has been extremely uncomfortable sleeping in cold, damp snow and squelchy mud. I have been kept awake lately by disturbing warning sirens. Will there ever be a day with a bit of excitement? I can't wait to get home to my dear parents and especially my loving and impatient dog, Bobbi. For now, I guess I will play cards to pass the time, waiting to get to my safe, beloved home.

Agatha Scrivens (9)

Ryhall CE Academy, Ryhall

The Bold Diary Of Lilly-Anna Banks

Dear Diary,

Today was crazy. I was putting on my usual lipgloss when it whisked me off to *Santa's grotto!* I was so confused because that had never happened before, but I just carried on wandering about until I heard a sound. I rushed over to see that Santa was struggling to get into his bright red coat. I took his coat and mended it and Santa was very impressed, so he told the elves about me. The elves taught me their ways and so I started helping them. That is how I started helping Santa and his tiny elves.

Holly Tinker (9)
Ryhall CE Academy, Ryhall

Moving House Mysteriously

Dear Diary,

Something tremendous happened to me. I was moving house and I went somewhere mysterious and sensational, it was magical. When we walked through our door I ate my dinner before I did anything. I decided I would do something else. I thought I had nothing, I looked in my wardrobe and it sucked me in.

"Hold onto your hat if you have one!"

I went into it and it had unicorns. I made friends with one. He was the nicest unicorn I had met but it was the first one. I woke up, I was dreaming.

Tallulah Sorbi (9)

Ryhall CE Academy, Ryhall

Who Were You?

Dear Diary,

Deep in a snow-covered world, I found an unknown creature. At first, I thought it was a cat, but no... a fox! I was very curious and puzzled. I loomed closer, it was glowing blue. As it came closer it looked sweet. Suddenly, it touched me and it gave me magical powers. I flew high in the air and ice shot out of my hands. In front of me appeared a beautiful gown and crown, I had never felt so alive. I turned to thank the magical creature but she had vanished! What a beautiful and interesting day!

Bella-Rose Ferreira (9)
Ryhall CE Academy, Ryhall

The Diary Of Dr Fishy

Dear Diary,

This morning, I swam 295m in 1.2 hours in the beautiful, elegant seas. After swimming, I saw Willy the whale and all of a sudden he ate me. Amazingly, there was my old lab inside him. Oh, Diary, I was so scared and shocked, but I love labs. There was a secret button and when I pushed it, I, Dr Fishy, assembled the *fishy army!* After a while, the super, amazing fishy army arrived at the midnight blue whale and the fishy army rescued me. We all escaped and we made it out alive! Phew!

Roman Epps (9)

Ryhall CE Academy, Ryhall

The Incredible Diary Of Lucky The Dalmatian Puppy

Dear Diary,

Today was both a sad and happy day. It started when I walked into a deep, dark wood. To be honest, I'm a stray, and, after a while, I lost my way. I shivered and shook and my tail went between my legs. I was lonely, anxious, and petrified. All of a sudden, there was something glowing and bouncing. I followed the magic ball to a beautiful cottage and magically the ball tapped on the door. An old widow answered. I got into a cosy and soft basket and we lived together happily ever after.

Ava Armstrong (8)
Ryhall CE Academy, Ryhall

My Weird Life

One stressful day I had to go to the hospital to meet my little sister because she had many problems and we were trying to get them cured. The next day I got detention for no reason. Two weeks later I graduated from secondary school but I felt A-Levels were too hard yet I still hoped to go to Uni.

When I turned eighteen, I got a scholarship for uni! A question I've always asked myself is, why does my life end up in dilemmas? Second, how come I get into trouble for no reason? Thanks for listening!

Esme Scholes (9)
Ryhall CE Academy, Ryhall

Fairy In Danger!

Diary,

You will never believe what happened to me today. I saw a fairy with gold, shimmery wings. At first sight, I could not believe my eyes, I even pinched myself twice to make sure I was not asleep. But sure enough, it was real. She only said her name, it was Emerald, very close to my name, Ellena. I told everyone at school but all they did was laugh at me, it was horrible. Later on that day, I saw her again and saved her from the neighbour's cat. And to say thank you, she spoke once again.

Ellena Burrill (9)

Ryhall CE Academy, Ryhall

Being Lost In New York

I was going to the airport today and it was really big. So we got to our plane and went to New York. We went to the shop in New York, it had so much stuff. I went out of the shop and I got lost. When I was lost, I was wandering around, I'm only nine, then I went to a food shop. The food was so expensive, a mango was thirty-four pounds and a banana was twenty-seven pounds. An apple was forty-one pounds and the total was one hundred and two pounds. But that was too expensive.

Tommy Chiverton (8)
Ryhall CE Academy, Ryhall

My Amazing Day Playing On My Nintendo

Today started like any other day. I had breakfast and asked Mum if I could play on my Nintendo. She agreed and I logged in, ready for battle. Suddenly, I felt an electric surge through my body and I was in the actual game! I realised the only way to get home was to play and win. Luckily, my friends were playing and with their help, I managed to defeat the enemy. Again, I felt the electric surge and I returned home just in time for lunch. Phew! This has been the best day ever.

Joseph Kettle (8)
Ryhall CE Academy, Ryhall

Aurora's Devastating Disaster Day

Dear Diary.

Today I wrote a poem about my disastrous day. I woke up warm and cuddly, I was to be fed. My rich tea sunk to its death. At the grip of my tea, all went dark. There was a power cut, so I went to the park. Riding my bike I fell. My siblings made me fight but I wanted to hold them tight. Busting from the tea, I ran to the loo but the toilet ate me. "Leave me be!" I cried.

I ran a bath because of all the faff, it was just right for me.

Aurora Penfold (8)

Ryhall CE Academy, Ryhall

The Lost Dog

Dear Diary,

Today my dog and I went to the park and we played in the snow and had fun. Fudge the dog went missing in the snow, he was only brown and the last time I saw him he was slipping, so I need you to help find him. I miss him a lot, so please help me find him.

Then, the next day I found him and he was licking me and hugging me. My dog now is home safely and he is playing now and all nice and safe. He still wants to play in the snow.

Noah Parnell (9)

Ryhall CE Academy, Ryhall

Footballer

I got up, had a breakfast of oatmeal and fruit then drove to the training ground and trained with the lads. This evening we had a match against Liverpool. I was really nervous about the match as it was a big game, and I didn't want to let down the team. The game started off slow but by the second half, it started to get exciting as I scored a hattrick, which helped us win the match 5-2. The boss was very happy.

Ashley Dawkins (9)
Ryhall CE Academy, Ryhall

Jurassic Era

Dear Diary,

A boy named Jole woke up in shock after he'd crashed into a boat. Jole was confused but he adventures into the lush, green woods. Jole had been walking for ages so he sat down on a rock. Suddenly, he heard a huge roar in the distance. Soon, he saw a large, crocodile-like face. Jole was confused but then the beast emerged from the bushes, showing its true form.

"Why are they all big?"

The creature roared fiercely.

"Argh!"

Jole began to run with the creature right behind him. Soon he reached a cliff. *Splash!* Silence.

Archie Jay (8)

Springfield Primary Academy, Scartho

Football Fan Changes

Dear Diary,

Once there was a little boy called Ralphie, all he wanted was to become the greatest football player in the whole world as that was his dream. Ralphie trained every day with his dad. His favourite team to watch was Liverpool. As the years went by, he got better and soon signed up for Liverpool. But also Ralphie was good enough to play for England in the World Cup final, and within the first fifteen minutes, Ralphie had scored the opening goal against Argentina. He'd gone on to score a hattrick, winning the game, bringing home the trophy.

Harvey Smart (8)

Springfield Primary Academy, Scartho

Magical Items

Once there was a little boy called Ben. He was capable of doing things by himself unlike his sister, Bella. Bella always asked Ben to do it instead, even if it was near her. One morning, Ben and Bella came downstairs and they sat down for breakfast. Ben said, "Do I have to go to school?"

"No."

"What?"

"You have to look after Bella, bye."

Bella felt dust up her nose and then everything in the house had eyes and a mouth and the objects were alive. At first, it was scary, but then it was fine.

Fearne Scott (7)
Springfield Primary Academy, Scartho

My Fantastic Avatar

Dear Diary,
My name is Summer and today I am going to tell you all about my Roblox avatar, so let's get started. Let's start with my name. My name is Winnieomg, do you like it? Next are my clothes, I wear a leopard print T-shirt and shorts. I also have some accessories like a scrunchy and also a headband. Right, what's next? Oh yes, it's my favourite game, that's probably all of them. I know, I know, it's not my favourite but it is worth it anyway. That's it for sassy Summer's fantastic avatar, hope you enjoyed it!

Summer Laker (8)
Springfield Primary Academy, Scartho

The Discovered Powers

Dear Diary,

Today was crazy! I was in my science class doing potions and my partner, Mia, threw an unknown potion on me. Suddenly, before I could blink, I felt weird, so weird I could faint. So that's what I did, I fainted. I suddenly woke up, then I figured that Mia threw a power potion on me!

"I have powers!" I screamed.

Everyone looked in disbelief, they laughed at me. Suddenly, an evil monster showed up. I stood up and started to stare, but then felt a sharp pain. Swords came out of my eyes and stabbed the monster.

Ella Pound (8)

Springfield Primary Academy, Scartho

The Secret Garden

Dear Diary,

I found something incredible, something amazing happened. I found a secret garden, it was beautiful, it had flowers and beautiful unicorns. I thought of calling it Uffington, it had vibrant colours. The next day I wore a dungaree dress that had big flowers on, and I then continued my journey. I found something unusual, there was another secret garden. This one was a nightmare, not like the dream one. It was full of cockroaches and spiders, it was spooky. I wanted to go back home, until I realised that I was really, really lost...

Aurorae Colley (9)

Springfield Primary Academy, Scartho

The Lost Princess

Dear Diary,

Today was the craziest day ever! Oh, sorry, I forgot to introduce myself. I'm Alex and my real name is Alexandra but I don't like it. Right, back to my day. It happened like this: I was watching TV and something came on the news. It was the marking of fifteen years since the newborn princess was stolen. She was called Alexandra and had a rare birthmark on her hand. Then I realised. My mum's study door was open, and inside I found it. The princess' stolen crown. Was I the stolen princess? My royal life awaits!

Ada Allan (9)
Springfield Primary Academy, Scartho

Ava The Adventurous Girl

One day there was a girl called Ava. She wanted to travel the whole of England. She lived in Ohio, but the place she definitely wanted to see was her friend's because when she went there last time she made a friend called Olivia. She asked her mom. Her mom said, "Yes."

So off they went and headed their way to England. After six hours they finally made it. Ava's mom called Olivia's mom to ask if Ava could see Olivia. Can you guess what she said? She said yes, so they went to the park together. What happy days!

Neave Bouch (8)

Springfield Primary Academy, Scartho

Alice In Her Magical World

Alice woke up in her soft, cuddly bed, and then she looked around her really clean bedroom. Suddenly, Alice and her bed teleported to another universe. Then... *Poof!* Next to the bed, on either side, were two fairgrounds, but Alice couldn't go on them because the bed was still moving. Then, when they moved up, there were two more! Then they saw a brown door and they went through it and it led them to space! They saw lots of planets like Saturn, Jupiter and lots more, but they couldn't see Earth, and at last, they were home.

Violet MacLeod (7)

Springfield Primary Academy, Scartho

Michael's Amazing Football Cup

Dear Diary,

I played against the best players in the world so I thought, *how am I going to win?* until there was backup. Fifty minutes into the game, there was a sudden injury. It was World Cup history. Messi scored. Jack equalised It went into penalties and it was a save from my keeper and then it came down to this. If I scored, we'd win, and... it was a *goal!* Top bins. To the final. And the score was... 5-4 to us.

So my manager said to me, "You lift the cup."

So my team went really loud.

Michael May (9)

Springfield Primary Academy, Scartho

Our Adventure In Space

Dear Diary,

You won't believe where I went in my dream last night! I went into space! I met my dog, Bella, and we dressed up like astronauts and whizzed around with no gravity. We saw Mars and got to control some rovers. We even sat on the moon and ate our sandwiches. Then we found a space shuttle. We entered our addresses into the space nav and it zoomed down like a big roller coaster through all the fluffy clouds. We made it back to bed, just before my alarm went off for school. *Best night ever!*

Love Martha.

Martha Cook (8)

Springfield Primary Academy, Scartho

Something That Cannot Be Explained!

It was in the woods. I fell, not really remembering what happened next. Well, that was until I woke up ten minutes later to find I was in a palace. *Where am I?* I thought, but it was then I remembered, I was running away from a two-headed dog. It was the exact same dog that was sitting next to the unfamiliar man smiling at me. I didn't understand what he said as my hearing was muffled. I rubbed my ear and found something... What was it? The Dream Master 2000!

"Yay, it's a dream! Yay!" I yelled happily.

Olivia Gibson (11)

Springfield Primary Academy, Scartho

Dear Diary

Dear Diary,

Today was the best day of my life! First thing we got to athletics and I came - oh sorry, I forgot, my name is Mae; I'm in middle school and I just got this diary yesterday. Oh right, back to my day. So I came first place and everyone cheered me on. I'm happy it went so amazing. Where was I? Oh yeah, so then after school finished, I went to a fancy restaurant and I loved it, especially the yummy ice cream. That was the end of my terrific day. That's all for now, well goodbye Diary.

Margot Allan (7)

Springfield Primary Academy, Scartho

Life On Roblox (And Defeating Jenna)

Dear Diary,

I'm Roblox Hacker. Today I played Donate Me and I got lots of Robux. First, I went onto the item shop and got a noob outfit. I was then called Roblox Noob. I had 1,000,000,000 Robux! I played Adopt Me. I got a mansion for 2,000 Robux that cost 4,200 Robux. I saw that after I slept on the bed in BedWars, all of my Robux had gone. I was really sad. Straight away I knew who it was, Jenna, the popular hacker. I had an idea. I hacked her account so I became Roblox Hacker. *Oof!*

Oscar Saxby (9)

Springfield Primary Academy, Scartho

The Diary Of The Eggcellent Easter Bunny

What a relief the day was saved. When I woke up, I was very excited because the time had come. It was time for my job which was to set up scavenger hunts because I'm the Eggcellent Easter Bunny. I hopped to many houses, then, with just one house to go, disaster struck. I glanced in my basket and I had no more eggs left. Whilst hopping around in a panic, I accidentally woke up a little girl called Sofia. Nervously, I managed to explain it to her and she very kindly gave me her Easter eggs to use.

Sofia Buckman (9)

Springfield Primary Academy, Scartho

The Green Person

Once upon a time, there was a girl called Nettles. One day, Nettles was in her garden with a drink when she put her drink down. The drink fell. It turned green. When she came back, she slipped and turned green. The next week she went back to school, the other children were nasty and mean. They picked on her, making her cry. This went on for months. Now she had no friends. One day, she was walking to school when she saw a group of kids laughing in a crowd. She went to look. Who was the blue boy?

Casey Goodwin (7)

Springfield Primary Academy, Scartho

A Mystery Mermaid

Dear Diary,

Today started as an ordinary day. Immediately after my lunch, I went to a mystery island to go camping. Lucy arrived a little later. During the night, I woke up restlessly so I took a walk and saw a glowing light at the side of a mountain. I made my way to the light and discovered a pool illuminated by the moon, a full moon! I got in and went for a swim. Then the pool started bubbling! I got out and it was morning. So we headed home. I got in the bath. A tail appeared...

Annabelle Balderson (10)

Springfield Primary Academy, Scartho

The Mythical Land

It was my bedtime but I didn't want to go to bed. So instead, I climbed out of my bedroom window and decided to explore. I was in my PJs so I had to change that. I got changed into my dress. I went out and discovered some woods. It looked really, really cool. I was walking a bit more and discovered a mythical land that had lots of sweets and unicorns. I ate them all up. Anyway, it was time to go home; I was really sleepy. Have a really, really, really good night's sleep too!

Evie Keeler (9)

Springfield Primary Academy, Scartho

Unicorns

Dear Diary,
I am Phoebe and I love unicorns. Today I will tell you what I love about unicorns. First, I love their silky mane and golden eyes. I also love the horns because they are different shapes and sizes and can be any colour like orange, pink, blue, purple, yellow and red, but they can still be multicoloured. They are my favourite mythical creature and I love them. I'm doing this in Unicorn Land and I am amazed to see all the unicorns.
Love from Phoebe.

Phoebe Wheeler (8)
Springfield Primary Academy, Scartho

Sadio Mané Versus PSG

Dear Diary,

I'm so excited, today's the big day. Bayern Munich versus PSG, Mané versus Messi, who will be the GOAT? Both teams are nervous. Mané runs down the wing and scores a trivela top corner and it's 1-0 to Bayern Munich. A few minutes later, Mbappé turns full Ninja Turtle and scores a volley outside the box. It ends 1-1 but nobody scores in extra time so it goes to penalties. Sané scores, Mbappé misses, Kimmich scores, Neymar misses, Gnabry scores, Messi scores, then Mané scores. Bayern Munich wins the Champions League. Messi retires and Mané becomes the GOAT.

Daniel Stonebridge (10)
St Mary's CE School, Norwood Green

The Cauldron Monster

Dear Diary,

Today was a very unusual day; I walked to school (in the rain!) at eight o'clock. At 8:15, I met up with my best friend, Lola. Later on, our first lesson was PE. Lola and I went to the PE cupboard because our teacher, Mr Fritz, asked us to get the ball for football. As we opened the glossy, light, brown door, there was this thing glowing, oozing with green. Lola told me it was a cauldron.

I shrieked, "A cauldron!"

"Lower your voice!" howled Lola.

A mysterious figure trotted towards us.

"Yes child, lower your voice!"

Millie-Sophia Carter Kapoor (10)

St Mary's CE School, Norwood Green

The Thing In The Sand

Today I went to the sea with my siblings. We felt something was a bit unusual because we were the only ones there, but we didn't think too much about it until we saw something in the sand. It started moving around and around, and then my siblings and I tried to pull it out of the sand.
Then we pulled and pulled then screamed, "Argh!"
Then the creature screamed too!
After we calmed down, we asked, "Who are you?"
The creature said, "I can make wishes happen but only for a day."
What happened next was shocking...

Aariya Sanghera (9)
St Mary's CE School, Norwood Green

The Tea Party

Dear Diary,

Today I had a tea party in Wonderland. I invited the Cheshire Cat, the White Rabbit and Alice. Cheshire Cat was the first to arrive. I gave him a biscuit.

Half an hour later we still hadn't had our tea as Alice and the White Rabbit hadn't arrived. I felt kind of worried.

Had they gotten lost? Were they hurt? Were they still asleep? There were so many possibilities.

Cheshire Cat seemed unbothered though. I heard a knock at the door and it was the queen, the White Rabbit and Alice!

What a relief. We drank our tea.

Kirsty J Bown (10)
St Mary's CE School, Norwood Green

My Brother

Dear Diary,

I have a brother called Jeriah and he's two years old. When I go to see him every other weekend I run to him and give him a hug.

When he sees me, he says, "Shanae, hi, I miss you." I say, "I miss you too, Jeriah!"

He shows me what he's done and what he's watching on TV. Jeriah loves watching Spidey and His Amazing Friends and his favourite characters are Spidey, Ghost-Spider and Spin. He loves them so much, he even copies the moves as well. Oh! I love him so much, he's the best ever!

Shanae Leo (10)

St Mary's CE School, Norwood Green

Diary Of Amazing Prime Hydration

Dear Diary,

I was introduced to the world on the 4th of January 2023, I'm Prime Hydration and who made me, you're asking Diary? KSI and Logan Paul made me. KSI and Logan have made nine flavours of me: Tropical Punch, Orange, Lemon Lime, Blue Raspberry, Mango, Ice Pop, Meta Moon, Grape and Strawberry and Watermelon. I also have an energy drink version and powdered Prime too. The bad thing: it's so hard for people to get me. Shops sell me for £1 and people sell it for up to £1000. But I am still happy with all the Prime.

Rayyan Mohammad (10)
St Mary's CE School, Norwood Green

Dear Diary

Today, Aunt Kate's cat, Boomerang, was snuffling in the massive old fireplace and disappeared through a gap. When Scott cracked it open, we saw a mini room. Then Jack went in and Boomerang jumped out. When Scott cracked it open again we saw a trapdoor. But where was Jack? Then we went down. In a chest was a scroll. What did it say? It said: 'The Keepers of the Key. We vow to uphold our pledge for the coming year. Carter, Goff, Nancarrow, White, Lugg, Tretherwick. In the year of our Lord 1755'.
What are they guarding? Who are they?

Isabella Rose (9)
St Mary's CE School, Norwood Green

Hero Kid's Adventure

Dear Diary,
One day I was drinking tea and I heard the villain of all villains was destroying Paris.
"Not for long because Hero Kid is here!"
So I flew to Paris, led everyone to safety and decided to face my foe. I got lots of confidence and fought until his army of villains came to attack me, but I just went invisible and defeated them. Then Megamind, AKA the villain of all villains, came, but soon the hero god called in all the heroes. With all of our power, we fought them. We saved another city that lovely day.

Aryan Dhiri (9)
St Mary's CE School, Norwood Green

A Trip To Go See A Satellite

Two people named Zack and Jimmy planned a trip to go see a satellite up close. They entered the rocket that would take them to space. The countdown started:
"5, 4, 3, 2, 1, *blast off!*"
Zack and Jimmy were very excited when they entered space, it was just like the movies. They set a course to the north to find a satellite, Tipton 4.11 with a famous scientist, Dr Cork Leafter. When Zack and Jimmy entered the satellite after six hours, they realised that they had to come back to Earth. What a day it had been.

Arnav Khandekar (9)
St Mary's CE School, Norwood Green

The House Disaster

Dear Diary,

Today was an unusual day as I was walking to the shop. I heard shouting and water flowing down the street. There was freezing cold water underneath my feet as the family ran out of the house. When the family came outside, people from down the road started to help get things out of the house. After all the things were out I heard unpleasant noises from the house! Five minutes later, there were really bad noises and then the house went crashing down! The owners were sad and disappointed because it was new and beautiful.

Ruby Joao (10)
St Mary's CE School, Norwood Green

Doodle Land

Dear Diary,

Today I woke up seeing different shapes, like... *doodles!* I *love* doodling. I doodle whenever I'm bored. Suddenly, my mum called me for breakfast. I headed off to school. School was boring! Science, maths, history and a SATs paper! Obviously, after school, I started doodling. I got back into a doodle portal and met a doodlecorn (a unicorn covered in doodles!). In real life, I was just sitting there, so my mum called me to go get a present for my friend's birthday party and it was amazing!

Esther Nang Htun Myo Aye (10)
St Mary's CE School, Norwood Green

The One Hundred Million Pounds Treasure Hunt

Dear Diary,

A few days ago, a stranger was just wandering around in our family business shop. He was just an unknown lad at first until he started telling his mythical and magical stories to us and the other folks, and he always asked for a glass of water, until one day he suddenly died and he was gone. We all mourned that day, but we decided to search his belongings and found an old treasure map covered in dust. Curiously, we rolled out the map and discovered there were one hundred million pounds of gold, so we set off...

Krish Nahar (10)
St Mary's CE School, Norwood Green

Fantastic Footballer

Dear Diary,
Another day as a fantastic footballer. It was fun and I scored a goal as usual. I feel energetic when I play, I enjoy it very much. The day I have a match I always make sure I'm ready to score a goal. Football is my favourite game to play, I find it very entertaining and also for me it's a hobby and I like playing football anywhere, anytime, any day. I have a passion for playing football, especially with my friends, that's what always makes me happy! Well, that's what it is, I need to go. Bye!

Zainab Akhter (11)
St Mary's CE School, Norwood Green

A Day In The Life Of A Spartan

Dear Diary,

Today was a tiring day. I am lucky that I survived. In the morning we were training and I nearly passed out in fear and fatigue. We woke up at 3am! My country was against the army of Xerxes of Persia. I am really disappointed. My closest friend, the one I've known since I was six, told King Xerxes of Persia about a mountain pass which led behind our line. King Xerxes imprisoned us. Thankfully, I sneaked away. I am currently hiding out in an abandoned mine. Wait, I hear many voices! Oh no! I need to hide!

Olivia Grace Parris (10)

St Mary's CE School, Norwood Green

My Wonderful Adventure

Dear Diary,

Today at school, I met a puppy named Poppy. She was very crazy and excited which made me excited too. We were both so stirred that we got tangled up in our leads! After we picked up our siblings from school, we went to a colossal green triangle (which humans call the green) where our siblings ran to a fenced area that had metal frames everywhere! Poppy and I both wanted to run so we yapped and barked until they returned. Poppy and I ran with our brother and sister until we reached the centre of the green...

Kyrie Schutter (10)

St Mary's CE School, Norwood Green

Into The Future

Dear Diary,

This was so especially amazing. I want to tell you about my trip to the future. So I was playing with my friends in the park when our frisbee landed next to an odd-looking bin that was making weird noises. I picked the frisbee up and decided to look inside the bin. To my amazement, there were lots of buttons and a small keyboard. It said on the top *Time Machine*. I gasped and jumped in. I knew exactly where to go in the future. I pressed a few buttons and it transported me into the bright future.

Leah Rai (10)
St Mary's CE School, Norwood Green

Life To Life

Dear Diary,
A girl named Mia was very excited because today was the day that she was going to space. She gathered everything she needed and soon she was off. When she was on the spaceship there were no errors. She came off the spaceship then four hours later she was off. This time there were errors and the spaceship fell into the waters. She passed out and then three hours later she was alive again. She was very confused by what had happened, but she could breathe.
She spent the rest of her life in the ocean.

Chidera Amako (10)
St Mary's CE School, Norwood Green

The Lover

Dear Diary,
I'm in love with a girl called Jenna Ortega, she changed my life. I had my BFF and it's Devika. She was the first person I told. I was a YouTuber so I made videos of her and got 289 subscribers. I was in love, I couldn't control myself. I was frozen every day thinking of her. She is an actor who works as the character Wednesday. I've never met her, she's 9 years older than me but I will try and meet her and keep her happy forever. I will give her what she wants. Goodnight, Diary.

Aaryan Mohan
St Mary's CE School, Norwood Green

Diary Of A Famous Frog

Dear Diary,

My name is Kermit, an aspiring actor. Recently, I made a movie about a superhero frog who defeats an evil lizard who tries to capture me, but I use my technology to defeat him and be set free. After we finished the last set, we hired some editors to finish up the movie. After a week, I got to see the movie and it was amazing! After a month, the movie was published and everyone loved it! The movie got millions of views in the first few days, and it was my best-performing movie ever! That's it!

Zau Lahkum-Lahpai (11)
St Mary's CE School, Norwood Green

Late For School!

Dear Diary,

Yesterday I had a dream. In my dream, I had superpowers and would go around saving people and pets. I finally earned some respect at school. I was having lots of fun and felt appreciated and happy. But then I suddenly woke up with a jolt, realising that I was late for school and that it was just a dream. Me being late for school is going to look horrible on my (already bad) report card, and then my parents are going to kill me... I have to go, my parents are calling me. I'll write more later.

Mysha Tasiq (11)
St Mary's CE School, Norwood Green

My Superpower

Dear Diary,

Today, I found out that I have a superpower (teleportation) and here's how it happened... I woke up at 8am and I changed my clothes, ate breakfast and went to school. When I went on the bus, I got stuck in *traffic! 8:40am, I am late for school! I wish I was there*, I said in my mind as I blinked. I saw that I was in school, sitting on my chair doing maths... I was so confused, what just happened? After maths, a thirty-minute break started, so I had to discover what it was...

Anastasia Sauch (10)

St Mary's CE School, Norwood Green

My New Mysterious Power

Dear Diary,

Hi, my name is Eliana Smith. I can't wait to tell you about my dream, or maybe reality, about how I may or may not have been able to read minds, and knew what everyone was thinking about. So it was just like normal when I ate dinner and fell fast asleep in my room. Then I woke up, but something felt weird. I went downstairs and I could see what my mom was thinking about. It wrote out 'work' and 'job'. Just then, I went to sleep. I wonder if it was real. But I was sleepy...

Eleonora Bahus (10)
St Mary's CE School, Norwood Green

Independence Day

I cannot go to school because this town is taken over by the Taliban and I'm forced to work as a farmer. I try to convince people to rise against the Taliban education system because they don't let children go to school. I think that's wrong. The other day I met an intelligent US soldier who had government connections and they told me that the USA are against the Taliban. They are trying to attack them. I will try to create a secret map to show where all their supplies are as I work as a farmer.

Samanpreet Singh (10)

St Mary's CE School, Norwood Green

Diary Of A Wimpy Kid: Prime

Dear Diary,

I wanted Prime, like so badly, so I hopped on my bike and went on a scavenger hunt. I went around the whole town to find Prime. Aldi, Sainsbury's and more. The next day it was a school holiday, I went to Italy so I searched every single corner there until I found Prime! I bought it for £10. I found out it was the last bottle of Prime in the world so I kept it in a container. People kept knocking on my door angrily until they stopped. I was so relieved that I sipped it.

Samuel Schiattarella (10)

St Mary's CE School, Norwood Green

Messi The Footballer

Dear Diary, the best friend,
The second-best player in the whole world is Maradona, but when he retired, Argentinian people got sad. Until Messi appeared. He had won a lot of matches for Barcelona. Then he joined the World Cup but he didn't win. He was not playing well so they started hating him for his worst game, but he finally won the World Cup for Argentina, and also he won the best player for the World Cup. Now Argentina supporters like him and Messi is remembered for his last World Cup.

Kerab Debela (10)
St Mary's CE School, Norwood Green

The Day I Got Lost In Time

Dear Diary,

On the 29th of February 2024, there was a little door in my room and when I opened it, a machine made a blue wormhole. Before I could react, I got sucked in. I heard weird sounds and then there was chanting and I saw England lifting the World Cup trophy, until some marshals grabbed me. Then I teleported to a temple and there were giants there. They were talking about destroying the Earth and I saw that one of them was Hades, so I ran and teleported home, but the door was gone...

Nathan Streets (10)

St Mary's CE School, Norwood Green

The Girl...

Dear Diary,

Hi, I'm Emily. My best friend, so-called BFF, is Evie and there's this girl called Anna. She bullied me in third grade, but my best, best friend that I was friends with for ten years has left me for the girl that bullied us. She's all happy, where is my happy ending? I followed all BFF codes, I was always there for her and now this is what I get. The anger burns my blood third-degree, and she doesn't even care that she hurt me. And I loved her so, so, so much...

Amelia-Rose Campbell Peccoo
St Mary's CE School, Norwood Green

The Wedding In India

Dear Diary,

Today is the first day of the wedding. I'm so excited to begin. First, we went in a carriage led by horses! It was so fun, we went through the whole street in a parade. Next, we had time to chill. We all played football in the hallway. We were looking out of the window and we saw a crocodile in the lake! Meanwhile, we got ready and we danced. We saw the outfits and they were shiny with pearls! Soon we had lunch, it was spicy but my cousins and I liked it. It was amazing!

Amaiya Chaudhry (9)

St Mary's CE School, Norwood Green

The Life Of A Football

Dear Diary,

It all started when a man kicked me and I fell over the fence and fell on the floor. Then someone picked me up and kicked me again and luckily someone caught me and kicked me again. They kicked me so high that he scored, then some other person got me out of the net and rolled me on the floor. I got so dizzy! After that, someone passed me between his legs and kicked me under someone's legs and I went in the net again.

"Goal!" everyone screamed...

Harjas Chopra (9)

St Mary's CE School, Norwood Green

The Best Tree

Today, while I was watching the children play around, a bird flew over to its nest. I thought that hopefully, a new bird might come (I am bored of the old birds right now!). Suddenly, a ball hit me hard! That hurt! But I knew the child did not mean it. Afterwards, it was time for the children to go home and for the birds to sleep. I don't sleep! After a few minutes, I saw a creature flying! It was a new bird! I made one of my branches really cosy to welcome the new bird when it landed.

Daria-Ioana Bobu (10)
St Mary's CE School, Norwood Green

The Great Adventure Awaits

Dear Diary,

My name's Kashish and I had a quest to complete. I was sent to the temple to transform into a lion with wings which was my gift from the gods. Then I began my quest. I arrived at a museum and saw a magical time machine. To do my quest, I had to find an ancient gem. So I zoomed through time in Egypt. I walked to the ruins of the temple. I used my power to sense the gem and there it was. A glittering stone which was the colour of emerald green. My quest was completed.

Kashish Yasin Mistry (11)
St Mary's CE School, Norwood Green

The Missing Potion

Dear Diary,

Yesterday, one of our special potions went missing! So, it all started when I was testing my potions, and then I saw on one of my potion shelves the Invisibility Potion was missing! I panicked a lot but luckily my friends Hermione and Ron were with me. All of us wondered, "What if Voldemort took it?" So, we quickly ran into one of the special chambers, but there were so many obstacles! I didn't know what would happen, but I knew it would be bad!

Nitya Itlas (10)
St Mary's CE School, Norwood Green

Fwoosh!

Dear Diary,
A school fire took place. I accidentally killed someone. I thought that was the end of me. Engulfed in flames, I was going to die, until... *Fwoosh!* My hand ignited into fire, but how was that going to help? It didn't. The opposite, in fact. I don't know why I'm still here, in fact. I ran out. My friend was so happy I made it out. He ran towards me. But he came to a touching distance and disintegrated in front of my very eyes. I stood there. Frozen.

David Daikri (11)
St Mary's CE School, Norwood Green

The Super Hedgehog

Dear Diary,

Tails and I went to stop the Doctor; he tried to take away the Gem of Life, so Tails and I had to go on a mission to save the Earth. If the Doctor gets the Gem of Life, something terrible will happen, and nobody knows what. Tails and I set off. Not knowing we had company, something red jumped at me and Tails. We were scared. I put Tails on my back and ran away. It was the Doctor's red monster. We got to the cave and stole the gem after I almost died. See ya! Bye!

Keziah Maqbool (9)

St Mary's CE School, Norwood Green

My Magic School!

Dear Diary,

Today I realised that my school is magic. I walked into Maths Room M and my teacher was flying. She told us to sit down but our chairs were floating! I was so scared! I ran out of class. When I looked at the clock, it was PE time. I ran into PE and my teacher turned into Ronaldo! I was excited to play football with him, but the bad news was that he won... but I got his signature. It was time for science. We were doing an experiment and mine blew up at home time! Ha!

Jessica Karolina Kwasnik (9)

St Mary's CE School, Norwood Green

My First Prime

Dear Diary,
Today I had a really amazing day. Today was the day that I ate a Prime lolly and drank Prime Ice Pop flavour. For both of them, they were so good, it was really hard to speak after eating and drinking Prime and now it is really hard to explain the feeling of it. It's just too hard to explain but I will try anyway. There was some flavour from the first sip and when I got the first lick of the lolly there was so much flavour. Best day of my whole, entire life.

Zaki Awan (10)
St Mary's CE School, Norwood Green

The Big Discovery

Dear Diary,

Today I discovered a bottle of Prime in a dark and scary cave. A door was behind it with litres of Prime. There were orange, blue, red, green, purple and black bottles of Prime. It was 100 feet underground and it was so cool and amazing. It was in a big safe, it was so hard to open. I made this my greatest discovery and it was so amazing and cool that I found this cave. Then I put the Prime discovery on the news and I got famous and went viral on the news. Yay!

Gurnoor Singh (10)

St Mary's CE School, Norwood Green

The No Clip Myth Of Hamboogars

Dear Diary,

I woke up from my coma, My name is Beefa and I live in a world where fast food eats vegetables. The day I woke up from my coma, I decided to kill our Hamboogaroos mafia. I went to French Fries Man so I could defeat the mafia with him. He killed the mafia. But it caused the rest of the fast food to go into a different world. Demon Nyan Cats were out to kill us, they were planning to make us burn in their pot of flames. One of them found us, we might die...

Joel Bhatti (11)
St Mary's CE School, Norwood Green

The Macaroni Crown

Dear Diary,

This is a day to remember, seriously! But to give you a hint... It might have something to do with mac and cheese. It started off at supper. I had to think of a way to dress like a king with what I had, for the school play! I had to be King Whirby! With a red shirt and sunglasses? I looked down sadly. I needed a crown... My gaze turned to my bowl of macaroni. If only I could stack it... It worked! Wish me luck for tomorrow.

Goodnight Diary, bye!

Limmy Tingneilim Khongsai (11)

St Mary's CE School, Norwood Green

My Trip To Dubai

Dear Diary,
I went to Dubai for two weeks, and on the third day, I went to a hotel called Atlantis. And it is the best hotel because it has golf, soft play and everything you could ask for. I stayed there for three hours, exploring with my dad, I loved it. I even got a slushie, it was mixed colours, raspberry and blueberry, delicious. Next time I go to Dubai, I will go to the Atlantis hotel to stay there for one or two days, it was the best time of my life. Yay!

Devika Thakrar (10)
St Mary's CE School, Norwood Green

The Magic Shell

Dear Diary,

Today I went under the sea to help the fish collect food for the winter. Then the sharks came to attack and take all our food. I swam to the bottom of the sea and I found a magic shell that had a note saying 'one wish', so I made a wish for the sharks to go away and they did. Then I helped all the fish collect all the food and I went home and played with my baby brother and watched a bit of TV, then I ate dinner: dinner, my favourite!

Radhika Kaupau (9)
St Mary's CE School, Norwood Green

The Power Of The Night Fury

I came from a distant realm, a peaceful place, but that soon changed when a dark plague came, turning my family to dust. But then the Dragon Queen took me in and taught me how to be a great warrior, but when I got my powers everything changed. I was sent to Earth to protect it (I mean that's normal, the world is usually in peril). Meanwhile, a wolf came to Earth at the same time. Soon we both changed into humans. And together we became an unstoppable team.

Ethan Hamlyn (9)

St Mary's CE School, Norwood Green

Mistaken Chocolate!

Dear Diary,

Today I woke up and felt like it was an ordinary Wednesday. It was Easter break and I was so ready to eat loads of chocolate! Then my sister and I went to the living room to discover where all the milk chocolate was. We looked for what felt like years, but we could not find it anywhere!

We woke up our parents and screamed, "*Where's the chocolate?*"

Then they whispered back and said, "In the fridge..."

Rafaella Armond (10)

St Mary's CE School, Norwood Green

The Day My Secret Gets Out...

Dear Diary,

When I woke up I never thought this would be the day everyone found out my secret. I went out with my friends late at night, not knowing it would be a full moon. I stared at it and then I started to change into my true form. My ears grew bigger and fangs and claws. I was a werewolf. The next thing I knew, we were surrounded by police cars. I jumped over them and ran into the forest behind the park, not knowing what I would do next...

Isla Mustafa (10)

St Mary's CE School, Norwood Green

The Orange Mango Prime

Dear Diary,

There was a new flavour of Prime and I saw it with my eyes. Then I knew I had to get it somehow because I had bought all the flavours of Prime and I thought that was the best drink. So I did the right thing and went to get the Prime flavour, but someone else got it and I wanted to get it but he got it first, but I knew I was getting that Prime no matter what! So I went up to him and then I woke up from my bed and I was dreaming.

Christopher Rodrigues (11)

St Mary's CE School, Norwood Green

The Half-Eaten Fruit

Dear Diary,

My sister told me about a king who had twelve wives and they all wanted a child. So later on, an old lady gave each of the wives one fruit and eleven of them ate the fruit and one of them left it out for later. A rat ate half, the other was what the woman ate. She had a half-baby, he grew up to be a hardworking man and one day he met the old lady who gave his mum the fruit and she made his legs grow back. It was a happy ending.

Sukhleen Deoora (11)

St Mary's CE School, Norwood Green

A Day In The Life Of Dwayne Wade

Get up 7am, join sons for breakfast. Meet team trainers at 9am for treatment. Start two-hour practice at 10am. Answer questions at media session after practice. Meet with business manager at 12:30pm. Head home around 3pm to catch up with sons after school, take quick nap. Get 5pm massage or acupuncture. Meet with stylist to discuss wardrobe for upcoming events. Dinner at 7pm. Catch up on favourite show, Scandal, before going to bed.

David Wilson-Paz (10)
St Mary's CE School, Norwood Green

The Secret Book

Dear Diary,

On a sunny day, I was in my bed when I heard a big bling-bling noise. I went to my cupboard and I saw the most incredible thing in my life: a magic book. I was so happy so I opened the book. I drew a burger then I got the burger. I was going to tell my mom but she would put it in the bin, so I kept it a secret. I asked it for lots of things, it was the best day of my life. I'm keeping it a secret secret!

Jahmala Joseph (11)
St Mary's CE School, Norwood Green

A PlayStation World

Dear Diary,

My friends (four of them) and I went to a forest to get some wood because it was cold and we needed to make a fire. We saw a blue PlayStation portal; we were scared and nervous but we took the risk and went inside. As we got through, my eyes glitched for a second. We were amazed! We noticed five TVs, five controllers and five sofas, enough for all of us! We felt enthusiastic!

Harman Chopra (9)

St Mary's CE School, Norwood Green

The Haunted School

Dear Diary,

I just found out the school is haunted. There was a shadow outside our window. The window's curtain was always closed. I felt quite suspicious. Then this morning, when I went to the toilets, the cubicle door was locked and the lights were turned off. The day before, there was a misty drawing saying *Kill*. I kept investigating and found out there was a ghost opening doors and closing them. I was so scared. Then in the girl's bathroom, there was a door that self-locked and blood on a book. I need to figure this out.

Signed Will.

Will J Frude (9)

The Erme Primary School, Ivybridge

The Disaster!

Dear Diary,

Today is my eighth birthday. It was a disaster. When I had got my delicious KFC meal, I turned around and suddenly tripped over my dad's foot. I went flying through the air and so did my meal. Chicken landed in people's hair and the beans rained down on the floor. As I got up, the whole restaurant was staring as beans dripped down my face.

Dad said very loudly, "It's okay, birthday boy." Suddenly, everyone started singing happy birthday. My face turned as pink as a peach and I cringed in embarrassment.

Henry Barons (8)

The Erme Primary School, Ivybridge

The Hooly-Hooly Man Lives In Our School!

Dear Diary,

Last night, when my friends and I were looking up our school on the Internet, you won't believe what we found... We found out that the Hooly-Hooly Man lives in our school. When we were scrolling down, we then realised that he lives in a girl's cubicle. This made a lot of sense because yesterday I heard about it in school but I didn't think it was real. Then, all of a sudden, we went to school the next day and in school it was weird, we heard knocking on the bathroom door. We wouldn't go in anymore...

Iyla-Grace Thorne (8)
The Erme Primary School, Ivybridge

Animal Experience

Dear Diary,
Today I was a hamster but I got myself in some trouble and here's how it started. I turned myself into a hamster but that's normal because I can turn myself into any animal I want. But that's not important, the important thing is that I got myself stuck in a house and an old lady mistook me for a rat. The old lady started chasing me with a spatula, trying to squoosh me with it. It was kind of fun because she kept on missing me, but then I got a wallop on my head.
"Ouch, stop!"

Layla-Mai Britton (8)

The Erme Primary School, Ivybridge

The Cake Disaster

Dear Diary,

On the eleventh of May, there was a disaster. It all began when my mum was making a Victoria sponge for my best friend's birthday. It was easy to walk there because we're neighbours. The cake had six layers of sponge, three layers of jam and two layers of icing. Then I walked to the house. I realised there were people already at the house. I walked up the steps and then fell onto the stairs and the cake went everywhere. I was also covered in the cake. Then I went inside with cake all over me.

Harry Turberville (8)
The Erme Primary School, Ivybridge

A Day As A Drinks Bottle

Dear Diary,

Today was the worst day ever as I woke up inside a drinks bottle. I heard that I belonged to a boy called Joshua. I heard from his class that he was a bit clumsy, so I just hoped that I didn't get broken! In the morning, it was fine as I was just sitting in the drinks bottle tray with other bottles. The next thing I knew was that everyone was going outside to play. After a while, they came back in and a big, slobbery mouth went around me. Urgh! I wonder what will happen now?

Nina Jewell (8)

The Erme Primary School, Ivybridge

The Birthday Disaster

Dear Diary,
Today was my birthday, I was turning ten. My friends made me a cake and it looked pretty. When I got to school, my friend hit the cake into my face. I did not like it at all. Then my mum and dad came in and sang happy birthday. I was so embarrassed! I ran out of the playground and into the bathroom but then I saw that it was the boys' bathroom. I ran out of the bathroom and out of the playground. Then it was finally home time, yippee! It was over now! Today was horrible!

Esmé Holmes (9)
The Erme Primary School, Ivybridge

Alphabet Day

Dear Diary,

My school has the alphabet law. At school, A played with his secret weapon while P was playing with G. F was playing with a shark whilst X was sitting at the table eating his breakfast. Then S began to play music to everyone. But B didn't like it, so he took the microphone off S's hand. When Q arrived at school, he put his backpack away and started to play with S and X. But then P and G arrived and with everyone they started to do the alphabet dance.

Ava Douglas (9)

The Erme Primary School, Ivybridge

The School Play Practice

Dear Diary,

Last week was the worst week ever because it was the school play practice, and there was this girl called Corrina Corrina. I was a shepherd and she was Mary, the one who made Jesus. The next day, it was the school play practice but little did I know, that it would be crazy. Corrina Corrina just arrived, my worst enemy. Oh no! Corrina Corrina was chasing me, she took me down to the floor.

Henry Bailey (8)

The Erme Primary School, Ivybridge

The Mermaid Who Saved The Ocean

Dear Diary,

On my way home there was so much litter everywhere. I saw a poor fish trapped in a bag so I freed it. I swam to tell my father, on my way I saw a litter picker at the bottom of the deep blue sea. I quickly picked up the cans, plastic, bottles and bags so no more sea creatures would get hurt. As a reward for cleaning the sea, the mermaid guardian gave me a guardian shark as a pet.

Elsie Hammond (9)

The Erme Primary School, Ivybridge

Jerry In Space

Dear Diary,

I was going to space. My name is Jerry. I needed to eat before I went and needed to pack some food and drinks. I felt excited to go in a rocket and see aliens. I got to space. I am also sixty-nine years old. I needed my outfit on. I landed on the moon. I could not fall because of gravity and I was jumping and it was fun. Then I got hungry and thirsty. Then I went home.

Bella McMillan (7)

The Erme Primary School, Ivybridge

Present Disaster

Dear Diary,

Last Christmas the worst thing happened. We got an email telling us the cake we had ordered over a month ago for a special occasion was lost. I felt embarrassed to turn up with no cake. What would she say? Luckily, they had lots of ingredients so we made a much better cake. It was delicious and it was a strawberry flavour cake.

Issy Croney (7)

The Erme Primary School, Ivybridge

A Moment At Lapland

Dear Diary,

One day, at Lapland, my brother pushed me down a snowy hill and I fell down onto my stomach. I acted like I was a penguin so I went down again and didn't want to leave. I would stand at the top of the hill and flap my arms like flippers. Then push myself down the hill, squawking as I went. Penguins have the most fun.

Freya Harper (7)

The Erme Primary School, Ivybridge

At War

Dear Diary,

Two weeks ago it was a war. I had a sniper with a twenty-magazine ammo pack. We were being bombed by German bombers. Luckily, we had tanks and we shot them down. Victory was ours. The Germans lost 200,000 soldiers whilst we only lost 600 soldiers. It was very scary. Sadly, my dad died whilst fighting the war with me.

Owen Rea Riding (8)

The Erme Primary School, Ivybridge

Triceratops Versus T-Rex

Dear Diary,

Sixty-six million years ago, a triceratops was fighting a T-rex and if you fought the T-rex, uh, well, you were going to die. The T-rex bit the leg and the frill and then the last thing the T-rex bit was the horn, but then the triceratops jabbed its horn into the T-rex and then the T-rex was dead.

Harry Hawkins (9)
The Erme Primary School, Ivybridge

YOUNG WRITERS INFORMATION

We hope you have enjoyed reading this book – and that you will continue to in the coming years.

If you're the parent or family member of an enthusiastic poet or story writer, do visit our website **www.youngwriters.co.uk/subscribe** and sign up to receive news, competitions, writing challenges and tips, activities and much, much more! There's lots to keep budding writers motivated!

If you would like to order further copies of this book, or any of our other titles, then please give us a call or order via your online account.

Young Writers
Remus House
Coltsfoot Drive
Peterborough
PE2 9BF
(01733) 890066
info@youngwriters.co.uk

Join in the conversation!
Tips, news, giveaways and much more!

f YoungWritersUK **🐦** YoungWritersCW **📷** youngwriterscw

Scan to watch the
Incredible Diary Video